# OFFICE PLAYER

## EDEN SUMMERS

# CHAPTER 1

"*B*eth, you're an asset to the Sutherland & Son team, but I'd like to make you a lot more than that. Much, much more."

Beth's brows jumped at her boss's words. He was old enough to be her father, yet his tone held an innuendo that definitely didn't scream fatherly intent as he leaned back in the plush seat, his fingers pitched over his chest.

This had to be a joke. Surely, any minute now, he would slap his hand on the desk, burst out in laughter, and say, "I'm joking. I'm not seriously propositioning you to be my mistress."

She pasted on a soft smile and tried to convey a calm that continued to elude her while she studied the gentle wrinkles of his indifferent expression. He scrutinized her, his head cocked, brows raised, waiting for a response. Fear bubbled deep in her belly, multiplying and turning until her stomach threatened to revolt.

"Umm…" She continued to frantically study him, taking in the firm set of his mouth, the slight raise of his chin.

Oh, God. He was serious.

She didn't need time to consider whether she wanted to be his dirty little concubine. The answer was a no-brainer—a resounding hell no—but she needed to handle the situation with care.

Her heart hammered as the walls closed in, her panic shrinking the room to a tiny box. The distance between them now felt uncomfortable and intimate, even though he still sat on the opposite side of his luxurious wooden desk.

Blood rushed in her ears and her chest grew tight. So damn tight. She needed to take a step back, clear her head, and wade through the crazy. She couldn't think under the pressure of losing her job, or her dignity, or hell, even her sanity. "Can we sleep on it?"

Max's lips fell open a crack. His blatant shock made her pause and do a quick rewind of what she'd said.

Holy. Crap.

"*Me*. I meant me...*alone. I* want to sleep on it—not both of us sleeping together." She pointed at her chest, trying to reiterate what her flustering couldn't seem to convey. "Not that I'm opposed to sleeping with you...I...just..."

Oh, no. Oh, no. Oh, no.

She needed to breathe, but her throat began to constrict. Her cheeks burned, and she hung her head in humiliation.

Where was her calm-under-pressure business persona? She tried to reclaim it, to paste on another smile and steady her gulps of air, but sadly, it seemed to have fled the building along with her boss's sanity.

Twelve years of city life and she still didn't relate to the loose virtues and low sexual standards of her city counterparts.

"I realize this is out of the blue, Beth, and I don't expect you to answer straightaway, but please take my offer into consideration. I think the arrangement would be mutually beneficial."

*Out of the blue?* Really?

*Mutually beneficial?* Oh, hell no.

She wanted to flick her wrist and wave away his comment. *No way, I receive similar offers from men twice my age on a daily basis.*

Instead of voicing the sarcasm, she nodded like a bobble-head on speed. "O-okay, Mr. Sutherland. I will definitely think about it."

She stood, taking an extra second to steady the tingling legs that threatened to buckle beneath her, before she retreated from his office.

Steve, her second in charge, passed her in the hall, his gaze narrowed with curiosity. "Everything okay?"

Her cheeks burned. The sordid details of the meeting felt like they were tattooed on her forehead for everyone to see. "Yeah, great. Perfect."

Super dooper awesome.

She rushed into her office, closed the door behind her, and let out a hearty sigh of relief. As soon as the breath left her lungs, she waited for calm clarity to return.

And waited.

And continued to wait.

Being a little optimistic, she gave it another try. A large inhale expanded her lungs, and then she counted to ten, letting it out.

Nope.

Not even breathing like a Zen master would calm her down. She needed to go home. Boarding the crazy train wasn't something she wanted to do in front of her colleagues. The team she worked with were friends, but the bastards stored up humiliating memories like they were lost treasures of Atlantis. At every available opportunity they would bring out their trove of memories to share.

She snatched her handbag from the bottom drawer of her

desk, contemplated the additional time needed to shut down her computer and decided against it. Seconds were ticking by and she didn't want to risk another encounter with Max today.

With her mind set in secret spy mode, she poked her head into the hall, taking a peek to the left and right.

The coast was clear.

She yanked her handbag onto her shoulder and stepped from her office on silent feet, closing the door behind her with a soft click.

As she pivoted on her toes to take the first small step toward freedom, she gave a routine glance toward Dean Sutherland's office. And froze.

*Shit.*

His frowning gaze held her immobile as he sat behind his desk biting the end of one of those expensive pens he loved so much.

Why, oh why, oh why did this have to be the only Friday in history that the boss's son didn't leave work early?

She straightened, gave him a crazy-lady finger wave with an overly-cheesy I'm-not-doing-anything-weird smile, and hightailed it to reception. Her muted footsteps moved from the carpeted hall to *tap, tap, tap* against the tiled floor of the waiting area.

The receptionist's back stiffened on Beth's approach, the woman's fingers madly clicking to close the pages on her computer.

"Looking at porn again, Ange?" Beth slowed long enough to fluster her too observant best friend.

Angela turned with a mock glare and pushed the headset microphone away from her mouth. "For starters, it's not porn. I'm looking at still images of the naked male form in all their blazing glory. I consider it art. And secondly, you know I hate how you sneak down the hall.

You're the only one here who doesn't walk like a baby elephant."

Beth wanted to laugh but she was sure the sound would come out as a sob. She smiled instead. "I'm heading home early. I'll call you over the weekend, okay?"

A crease marred her friend's forehead. "Everything all right?"

No, not at all. Thoughts of her boss flashed through her mind. Unwanted images of Max's naked body as he gave her a come-hither glance.

She had looked up to him like a father figure. Apparently, he had looked up to her, too, but his comparison was probably closer to the way a guy gazed up at a dancer working a stripper pole.

She shivered, trying to dislodge the horror. Could a man his age actually get it up without chemical intervention?

Of course he could.

The more important question was—why the hell was she even pondering the functionality of his dick?

*Christ.*

She would need to scrub her brain with a toothbrush and bleach if she ever wanted her libido back.

"Beth?" Angela's voice held a hint of concern. "I asked if everything is all right?"

Beth reached the elevator and pressed the button. She needed more distance from her friend's perceptive gaze before she turned back to answer.

"I'm fine." She cringed at her unnaturally animated tone and mentally forged ahead with a beaming grin. Great, now her friend would know, without a doubt, something was wrong. "I'll call you tomorrow."

The merciful elevator arrived before she could display more of her deplorable acting skills. She hustled inside, mouthed a silent prayer of thanks to the gods of impeccable timing, and pressed the button to the lobby, getting her ass as far away as possible from the much older man who wanted to get in her panties.

The plan had been to go home and drown herself in a bottle of wine. An expensive bottle. One capable of causing memory loss because forgetting this afternoon sat high on her agenda. But twenty minutes later, she was still in the building, seated on a stool at the sports bar located on ground level.

The world resembled a much better place now. In the space of a few quick shots, her awesomely crappy day flittered away like fairy dust in a snow storm.

All her troubles faded, moving from her mind with each drink until they became snagged on thoughts of her boss.

She swiveled her stool and surveyed the room to keep occupied. Small groups of people mingled, laughing, drinking, while taking complimentary food off trays located along the polished bar.

In a few hours, the majority of the Sutherland & Son employees would be here, enjoying the tradition of Friday afternoon drinks. She needed to leave before they arrived, but at the moment nobody paid her attention. The only person to acknowledge her since she'd walked in had been the bartender.

She turned back to hover over her empty shot glass and stared into the clear liquid, wondering why her life had taken such a bad turn. Her career had always been demanding. Every day brought new issues to deal with or another task which required urgent attention.

That was the thrill. She loved the fast-paced environment.

It was hard work, plain and simple. Being product

manager of one of the biggest electrical appliance manufacturers in the country wasn't meant to be easy.

The sexual harassment, however, was a whole new hurdle she hadn't anticipated. An unwanted *bonus* to her workplace agreement. But she wouldn't let the drama ruin her fast track to success by suing the company.

*Suing.*

She sighed and threw back the vodka shot in one gulp. The start of the week had been all about kicking butt and taking names. Now, she was the one getting her ass kicked while legal proceedings hovered in the back of her mind.

She lifted her empty glass to gain the attention of the bartender and smiled at him to request another.

Moments later, he slid a filled glass toward her, a flirtatious grin tilting his lips. She should totally go there—to the hot and sweaty place his twinkling blue eyes alluded to—except she didn't do one-night stands.

Every one of her sexual experiences held an emotional commitment, some form of bond between her and her lover, and no matter how much of a hunk the bartender was, a cocky smirk wouldn't cut it.

Instead, she ignored his interest and mumbled, "A vodka and Coke, too, please."

She needed a chaser. Her mind still craved enough alcohol to make her incoherent, even though her body hummed with a warning to slow down.

The way she swayed on the stool was a great indication she should listen. Four shots—three more drinks than her weekly average—and she was already close to tanked, yet the image of Max Sutherland's hands on her naked body wouldn't quit. She couldn't stop reliving the meeting, analyzing it, cringing over it.

In all honesty, the shots were probably exaggerating her tension. Her boss wasn't a horrible man. He ran his business in a fair and honest manner. His looks weren't all that bad either, an older version of his son's aesthetic perfection. She would probably consider him attractive if she went for older men…much, much, older men. But he was her employer, and twenty-five years her senior, for God sake.

Max hadn't even suggested the offer in a flirtatious or enthusiastic tone. He pitched it like a business proposal. As if outlining the benefits of the latest kettle on their assembly line. Maybe if the proposition had been stated in an enticing manner she would have felt flattered instead of icky.

The bartender slid the vodka and Coke her way, the suggestive smile and gleam in his eyes still in full force. Before she could thank him for the drink, his focus drifted to the low neckline of her blouse and became trapped in her cleavage.

Was something in the building ventilation making everyone infatuated with her today?

She contemplated gawking at his zipper and the slight bulge in his pants continuously for the next half hour. Then he would realize the error of his ways. Scratch that. With the current sparkle in Mr. Pretty Boy's eyes, he would probably consider it a come-on, and she didn't have the focus to give him the verbal smack down he deserved.

Clearing her throat, she tilted her head to the side and raised her eyebrows until his baby blues climbed to meet hers. Their gazes met, and he had the nerve to give her an arrogant smirk before moving to serve another customer.

Asshole.

This swas exactly why she didn't enjoy drinking with the yuppies in the central business district.

"Don't hold it against him. It's hard not to stare at a woman with your beauty."

The familiar, husky tone had her back snapping ramrod straight. Her heart shot to her throat and her nerves tingled in hyperawareness. Through her periphery she watched Dean Sutherland take the stool beside her. All sophisticated and confident.

Great, exactly what she needed. She didn't bother to look at him, knowing in her current state she would stumble across the line of professionalism, plummeting headfirst over the cliff of lust if she focused on those dark chocolate irises.

She let out a deep breath and tilted her head to the ceiling to pray for guidance. The air continued to leave her lungs as she grabbed her drink and threw it back in quick, choking gulps.

Of all the people, in all the bars, in the entire city, Dean had to be the one to approach her. Admittedly, the sports bar *was* located at the bottom of their high-rise office building, so it was inevitable that a colleague would spot her—but did it have to be him?

The sexy, smart-ass took pleasure in unwittingly teasing and taunting her on a daily basis. Every moment in his presence reminded her of the feel of his sultry lips against hers. Their one alcohol-filled embrace from last year played on a continuous mind loop—perfect and perfectly stupid in equal measure.

Now he sat beside her, talking about her beauty as if he actually believed the compliment. Too bad she wasn't convinced by a single word of it. She refused to falter.

All they had was playful banter. Nothing more. And their so-called professional relationship definitely didn't allow for the luxury of letting him see her in this state—swaying on her stool in a complete mental mess.

The cherry on top of her perfect afternoon included the inability to bitch to him about the scandalous meeting. Max Sutherland may be the managing director of the company, but Dean was part owner, and a director himself. It didn't seem like a great career move to bad-mouth the boss to his own son.

"What do you want?" Her agitated words came out with a tiny drunken slur.

He raised his finger to the bartender, self-confidence ebbing off the material of his expensive charcoal suit. "Scotch on the rocks, thanks."

The bartender gave him a nod and began to prepare the drink. Dean turned his body toward hers, the hardness of his knee bumping her thigh leaving a scorching trail along her skin. "I was walking by and caught sight of you at the bar. You fled the office in a hurry. I wanted to make sure everything went okay in the meeting with my dad."

Her heart fluttered even though she knew his concern was nothing more than idle conversation.

At one time, she would have cherished the thought of him caring about her, but after months of watching him with a revolving door policy on women, she knew he was incapable of monogamy.

Dean was a player. A self-assured man, proud of his womanizing ways. He could make women pole dance in the palm of his hand with a mere glance. Hell, he could make *her* pole dance in the palm of his hand at a time like this.

She swiveled toward him, needing the visual to confirm whether his concern was genuine or a tease.

His face held no humor. His usual casual appearance was now troubled with a set jaw and creased brow. The taunting amusement she heard in his voice earlier had disappeared from his expression.

"Everything's fine." She spared a moment to appreciate his appearance before she turned back to the bar.

From his Italian leather shoes, all the way up his expensive tailored suit, to the casual shaggy haircut, he was a mighty fine specimen. She couldn't be ashamed of the heated attraction running through her veins. Nobody could deny he was undeniably gorgeous. And she certainly couldn't pretend he wasn't a phenomenal kisser, too. He just didn't deserve any more female attention.

The man's ego could overflow a football stadium and the women he slept with could fill all the seats.

She had practically drooled the first time they met, with the haphazard way his hair fell to highlight those dark eyes. The healthy tan and athletic physique only added fuel to her eagerly blazing fire.

Now, he sat beside her, his leg brushing hers, and she wondered what other great assets he had to offer under all those expensive clothes.

To occupy herself, she mentally counted the liquor bottles lining the wall behind the bar. Her count reached two before her concentration shot to hell and her gaze caught his reflection in the wall of mirrors behind the display shelves.

Her vision followed his strong cheekbones, moved down the corded muscles of his neck, over the opening of his business shirt while his head tilted back as he drank.

Their gaze met briefly in the mirror, his heated, hers surprised, before the connection shattered when he slammed his glass down with a thud.

"Come on. We're leaving." He threw money on the bar and shoved off his stool.

"Excuse me?" She swiveled toward him, her brain needing extra seconds to catch up as it struggled to swim through the liquor.

"I said, *we're leaving*. Get up. I'm taking you home." His words were calm, firm, and in complete contrast to the stormy expression in his eyes.

"No." She turned back to the bar, intent on gesturing for another shot. Not that she needed more liquor. Her head already buzzed. But she knew it would piss Dean off and for some reason that task had bumped to the top of her agenda.

As she lifted her arm, a firm hand encased her wrist. She gasped, and anger hardened her expression…until the heat from his touch brought a spark of awareness she didn't appreciate.

It had taken months of determination to forget the kiss they shared almost a year ago. A kiss that blew her mind and left her achingly vulnerable, yet hooked on his effortless charm.

She couldn't stand to be another face in his never-ending line of women. To sleep with him but mean nothing to him emotionally.

Self-preservation demanded she step back, to maintain professionalism. To also keep her job and her sanity.

So, that's what she'd done for endless months. Dean's sexy bedroom eyes and husky voice had tested her resolve on a daily basis. Now, his fingers touched her, and the alcohol made her question whether it meant more than common sense suggested.

She glared at the hand holding her wrist. "Let go of me, Dean."

He moved forward. Close. *Too* close.

His breath warmed her neck and sent a shiver through her chest. "You're making a scene. If you haven't already noticed there's a table full of my father's business associates behind us. Now, unless you want daddy dearest to tan your ass for acting unprofessional, while still technically within business hours, I suggest we leave."

The visual of Max spanking her made blood rush from her head. Goosebumps covered her skin as she pulled herself out of the horrific vision. She glanced over her shoulder and confirmed his words. In the corner of the room sat a table full of Max's associates, thankfully engrossed in drinking and conversation.

"Come on. I'll drive you home."

She inched away, his fingertips scorching a trail along her skin—over her wrist and down the sensitive area at the back of her hand. It felt like a caress. A deliberate provocation. And she had to close her eyes to fight for composure.

A lift home might be for the best. The train was scary enough when sober, let alone hyped up on this man's lingering touches.

Ignoring the soul-shattering jolt his physical contact evoked, she straightened and tried to focus on the way the ground wavered. Walking would be a difficulty she hadn't anticipated.

She cursed the polished floorboards and her love of stiletto heels as she took the first step.

The ground moved like a water balloon under her feet, her heel losing traction as she fought for balance. She grasped for anything within reach so she didn't land on her ass, and came up with Dean's arm.

His strong as steel arm.

She clung to him with the force of an eagle's talons, unwilling to let go and gracelessly drop to the floor.

The superior smirk he fixed her with spoke volumes, making her wish she gripped him for reasons other than her drunken stupidity.

A blush burned her cheeks as she gave a tight smile and righted herself. "I'm fine." She patted away the hand trying to keep her steady. "Just practicing my dance moves. That one was called the baby giraffe."

He chuckled, the deep melody washing through her like a gentle stream. "Yeah, clearly you've got the moves like Jagger."

# CHAPTER 2

*D*ean led the way onto the busy sidewalk of the Melbourne CBD, resisting the urge to lean into the long, blonde hair cascading over Beth's shoulder. Something sweet, entirely feminine, and uniquely *her* filled his lungs. If he tilted his neck a little, his face would be surrounded by the mass of golden strands swaying in the late spring breeze.

He tried to shake the infatuation, instead concentrating on guiding her around the throng of people as they headed toward his car parked a block away. He held her steady, resting his hand on her waist while he walked her through the traffic.

When her steps faltered, he swore aloud. His eagerness to keep her upright sent his hand gliding under the fabric of her suit jacket to land on her silk blouse.

The delicate material barely formed a barrier against the pliant, tender flesh underneath, and the last thing he needed was more temptation.

He felt like a damn teenager, his cock already on standby,

poised, eager, and readily available to commence the launch sequence at a second's notice.

He frowned, wondering how the hell he would get her home without making this more awkward. Obviously, offering her the walking stick growing from the crotch of his pants wasn't a good idea.

And even if they did have that sort of playful relationship, her snappy mood was a great indicator she wasn't in the mood to joke around. All he could do was pray she remained reasonably sure-footed in those tiny black heels for the next block. Then he would gain some space.

But that didn't help with the nagging need to know why she was emotional in the first place.

Even when frustrated at work, Beth still had a soft smile for everyone. She wasn't high maintenance, didn't crave attention, and rarely showed weakness in any form.

She didn't usually drink much either, not even at work functions—well, not since one memorable kiss a lifetime ago —and he'd never seen her drink during work hours. Ever.

He hated seeing her like this. His temper spiked with the possibilities that could have arisen from a private meeting with his father. If the matter was personal, her best friend Angela would have given him the heads-up, but the receptionist had been clueless.

He didn't even know how much she had to drink, but her glazed expression indicated she'd been generous in her consumption.

She shuffled forward, leaning harder into him. "You smell so good," she moaned into his neck.

Yep, she was definitely trashed.

"Beth." His tone held a warning as his cock twitched. He would need a damn leash on his dick if she didn't settle down.

Daydreams already clouded his judgment. Images of dirty

things in darkened alleys made him harder by the second. If she moaned in his ear again he doubted he would be able to resist the urge to lean her against the closest building and take her mouth. Hard and fast.

"No, really." She rested her head on his shoulder, her hair splaying over his chest as her footing straightened out. "You always smell so good. It's infuriating."

He suppressed a groan and directed her around the last street corner, heaving a sigh of goddamn relief when he spotted the parking garage.

He paid extra money to have his car stored on the ground level, close enough to the attendant's booth to be under constant supervision.

There was only a few more yards until freedom. A few more steps until thankful space. A few more heartbeats before he could move her pliant body away from his and regain his ability to think clearly.

"Why do you have to smell so good?" she grumbled. "As if being smart and sexy wasn't enough, you have to smell all masculine and dreamy. It's an unfair distribution of assets."

The compliment didn't surprise him.

The woman saying it did.

It wasn't a secret he found it effortless to score with the ladies. Women seemed to crave his power, along with his bank balance. He just assumed Beth was immune.

The vain women of society, the spoiled heiresses, the air-brained models, yeah, they all wanted to be with him, but Beth didn't look at him too much anymore.

Intoxication was well and truly doing the talking.

"Sexy, am I? I bet you'll regret saying that on Monday morning." He tried to downplay her words, hoping for a change in subject.

Self-control didn't sit high on his list of favorable quali-ties, and at the moment, it barely registered in his vocabulary. If she continued to test his resolve, he would either make the mistake of seducing her or have to end the night with a bag of ice on his balls.

Neither option was enticing.

"What?" She turned her head toward him.

Those big green eyes pierced his soul, making him ache from the tips of his fingers to the arches of his feet.

"As if you didn't know. That's the one thing that pisses me off about you, Dean Sutherland; you're too arrogant. If it weren't for that ego of yours…"

*What?*

His chest tightened with the need to ask. Instead, he ground his teeth and tried to convince himself her words meant nothing in her drunken state.

He strode into the parking garage and gave a wave to the attendant in the compact booth. His black BMW Z4 sparkled like the night sky, even in the dreary light. His ride was the only stable female in his life—beautiful, reliable, and faithful.

Perfection.

He released Beth's waist and moved to open the passenger door. She wobbled, teetering on her heels, and he cursed his stupidity for not warning her first.

"Shit." He slid toward her, trying to steady her by pressing his body into hers. He gripped her hips, their bodies molded so close his growing erection rubbed against her abdomen.

She stared at him, those beautiful eyes filled with interest. The world fell silent around them, their rasped breaths the only noise…except for his hard cock crying for attention between them.

"Sorry," she whispered. Her clawing fingers clung to his shirt. "I'm really not *that* drunk, just more than a little clumsy today."

He swallowed, hard, and distracted himself by trying to recount how much money he lost on the last Melbourne

Cup. He needed to move away, to take a step back from the friction heating his body and the blatant attraction in her stare.

She had to stop looking at him like that. With wild eyes filled with palpable desire capable of destroying him one slow inch at a time.

Her hand rose, her delicate fingers running through the hair around his face.

*Christ.*

Every nerve in his body buzzed on full alert. His scalp tingled. Goosebumps cascaded down his spine. And then there was the throb in his groin that wouldn't fucking quit.

The woman continued to undo him with her eyes, her touch, her need, and he couldn't do a damn thing about it.

If she were sober, he wouldn't have a second thought about leaning in to kiss her. He would slant his mouth over hers until they were breathless. Mindless. But she wasn't.

Beth was drunk and dealing with issues he hadn't had a chance to discover yet.

He narrowed his gaze, planning to say something cocky, something arrogant and egotistical to annoy her into backing off. But then she had to go and smile at him. A slow seductive curve of lips that brought out two tiny dimples and made his breath catch.

She didn't give him a chance to speak before her hot little tongue snaked out to wet her plump bottom lip, making it glisten in the fading light.

Who the hell was this woman?

The Beth he knew was sassy and as sharp as a spitfire when they verbally sparred. In contrast, she was always professional and usually a little reserved when it came to things of a sexual nature.

She would flirt and tease on occasion, batting those long lashes with exaggerated femininity when she needed his help. But he hadn't seen the spark of interest in her eyes since their kiss. And he refused to let history repeat itself with another drunken regrettable moment.

Last time, the night had started off simple, with the company's usual end-of-week drinks in the downstairs bar.

He remembered being surprised to see her with a glass of wine in her hand. She even teased him with suggestive glances that made him lose all self-control. The well-mannered woman had turned into more of a playful hellcat with each sip of sparkling liquid.

When people started to wave their goodbyes, he had offered to take Angela, Steve, and Beth to Onyx, the newest club in the city. He told himself he only wanted more time with her. Some personal one-on-one out of their working environment, to see if the connection between them was more than mere office flirtation.

Seduction hadn't been in his plan.

He wasn't willing to risk the relationship they already had. But Angela had seen through his denial and pulled him into one of the darkened recesses of the club's entry hall to tell him in no uncertain terms she would castrate him with a dull knife if he hurt Beth in any way.

The caution hadn't been necessary. Beth had meant something to him. He hadn't been sure what that *something* was. But it wasn't a mere itch. Until he downed a few more drinks and she turned into a temptation he couldn't resist.

The four of them had scored a booth in an obscure corner to the side of the main bar. Although there had been enough room for all of them, Beth remained standing, her eyes focused on the dance floor, her body swaying to the beat of the loud music.

He'd been riveted on the way the lights glimmered in her eyes; the way each song brightened her smile. On occasion, she would glance his way, her teeth biting into her lip, then as quick as she turned to him she would look away, a flush heating her cheeks.

He remembered thinking it would be a mistake to get involved; to risk their friendship to satisfy his need to taste her. But the alcohol buzz had worn down his rational thinking, letting the dictator between his legs take hold of the reins.

His feet had moved of their own volition, coming to a halt in front of her. And before he could stop himself, he was leaning into the warmth of her body, asking her to dance.

The loud beat of music hadn't compared to the *thump, thump, thump* of his chest when she shook her head, rejecting his offer.

He hadn't expected the cold shoulder. Women usually begged for his attention and being turned down by Beth made it even harder to handle.

He camouflaged his disappointment with a friendly smile and a shrug, then he gave the excuse of buying the next round of drinks so he could lick his wounds in private.

When he turned to leave, she stopped him, gripping the lapels of his suit jacket. Her eyes searched his in hesitation, the noise from the club fading away as she slowly pulled him forward.

There hadn't been time to think. Her unsure innocence caused him to react. He wrapped his arms around her, one encompassing her waist, the other gripping her neck. Tilting her head back, he aligned their mouths and peered into her eyes with knowing intent.

He battled to control himself, needing to give her a moment's hesitation to pull away.

She didn't.

She fucking didn't.

Beth gripped his lapel tighter in one hand, the other snaking around his neck, stopping to tease his nape by digging light fingernails into his flesh. The hint of perfume tormented his senses and instinct led him to tilt his head into her neck. He nuzzled at the silken skin, her essence consuming his lungs.

He nipped once, grazing a path with his teeth up to the sensitive place below her ear. A needy moan escaped her lips, her alcohol-sweetened breath brushing his face. Her head nuzzled into his, searching, seeking, and he didn't second-guess pulling back slightly before moving in to taste.

The first caress was featherlight, smoother than silk, as her mouth moved against his. He swept his tongue along the seam of her lips, needing more, and enjoyed the way she granted him access. Her fingers ran through his hair, lightly tugging, spurring him to new unrestrained heights, turning him wild. Savage.

He stepped into her, grinding his erection against her pelvis, wanting her to feel his desire, needing her to know the way she affected him. She moaned, kissing him back with simmering heat. Her tongue tangled with his, the soft tentative strokes making the desire to grind against her unbearable.

No kiss had ever been sweeter, no woman more hypnotizing, and drunk or not, no one had ever affected his heart the way she did.

When she abruptly jerked back, turning away, he hadn't known what to think. Not until the lust in his veins slowed and the blood roaring through his ears dulled to a lazy rush.

Angela and Steve had been watching. Wolf whistling. Yelling.

The regret in Beth's eyes had damn near killed him. He was furious with the need to brush away the heat in her cheeks. To lean in and tell her it was okay. But she transformed in an instant, straightening her shoulders and sobering with the speed of light.

Five minutes later she was gone, leaving with nothing more than a wave and a rueful glance.

Instinct had demanded he chase after her, but Angela stopped him.

*Give her space. I know she cares for you, but she hasn't been with a guy in a while. And you're her boss. She needs time to think it through.*

He'd made the stupid decision to let her go, giving her the weekend to think it over. During that time, his hopes had grown.

He imagined them moving forward, maybe dating. *Yes, dating.* He had to get to know her out of their work environment. But Monday morning had been a bitch slap of reality.

Beth had done a complete one-eighty. The flirting had stopped, along with the playful banter, to the point where she would only communicate with him on a strictly professional level.

It had taken months to wear her down, to get their relationship back to where it had been before the kiss.

So, right here, right now, he had no plan to fuck that up with another drunken moment.

"Beth, you're extremely inebriated—"

She laughed, the feminine sound tickling his skin and shooting his restraint into dangerous territory. "Extremely inebriated? Seriously, Dean, who talks like that?"

He bit back a growl, hating the need to be the responsible one. "I do, when I'm trying *damn* hard not to take advantage of a friend while she's drunk."

Her eyes widened. Her mouth fell open.

He glanced away before she replied and occupied himself by making sure she was steady on her feet. After he convinced himself she wouldn't fall, he stepped away to open the car door, moving with a speed Superman would envy.

"Get in." His tone was harsh, the devil on his shoulder

poking him so hard he wanted to punch his fist through the car window.

*Just kiss her.*

*Fist those silky locks.*

*Tame that sassy mouth.*

He clenched his jaw as he helped her into the car and fixed the seat belt in place. Once she was settled he closed the door, turned his back on the car, and tried to pull himself together.

*Breathe, just fucking breathe.*

She was drunk, for God's sake, and he wasn't a horny teenager anymore. He could handle his dick.

This was the perfect time for him to finally grasp a moral compass and do the right thing where a woman was concerned.

Normally, he did easy conquests, and the easy conquests he spent time with didn't know the meaning of morals. He had his father to thank for that. The old man ruined his opinion on the opposite sex, not to mention his outlook on love and all that cuddly, emotional shit.

Until Beth.

He'd never wanted a woman as much as he craved her. Since his father had awakened him to the bite of female betrayal, there hadn't been a pull stronger than sexual attraction toward anyone.

What he felt for this woman was a hell of a lot more. She made him second-guess his opinion on commitment and made him want something he wasn't sure existed.

Unable to put off the inevitable, he walked around the car and paused at the driver's side door. He took one last calming breath and begged for his cock to settle down, then yanked the door open and slid inside. Without a word, he belted up and became instantly enslaved by the smell of her perfume.

*Fucking. Hell.*

He had to breathe through his mouth to stop her intoxicating scent from dragging him under. There was no escaping her. No escaping *this.*

*No.*

He was in control. He could get her home without defiling her. No problem. He would drive her straight there, do the gentlemanly thing and help her inside. Then he would leave, hotfoot it to his house, and spend the rest of the night trying to kill the ache in his groin.

"Where am I heading?" He watched her movements through the corner of his eye.

She turned to face him, her head resting lazily against the leather seat. Her voice was sultry as she relayed the address, so damn flirtatious he couldn't hold back from hammering his finger against the GPS while he programmed in her details.

He wanted to sob like a little bitch at the injustice of the situation—Beth drunk and willing in his car while he sadistically stuck to the moral high road.

This couldn't be happening.

It *shouldn't* be happening.

All it would take is one lapse in judgment and they could both be deliriously sated. At least until tomorrow.

He tightened his hands on the steering wheel and watched his knuckles drain of color.

He would be fine. He just needed to keep himself occupied. Once he got home, he could relax with a few beers, enjoy some adult entertainment to numb the thought of her, and have a one-on-one session with Mrs. Palmer.

*Fuck.*

He hadn't needed to jerk off this bad in years.

# CHAPTER 3

*B*eth shamelessly stared at him the entire trip home. She memorized the way taut muscles ticked across his jaw, how his strong, tanned hands gripped the steering wheel. The way his deep breaths expanded his broad chest, and the major tent action in his pants.

That tentage was damn impressive. The elevation alone could shelter a family of five.

She continued to stare, imagining the size, the taste, the texture… When clearly she needed to retrieve her mind from the gutter before she started to drool.

Oral sex had never been her forte. Right now, though, the desire to take him in her mouth, to lick and suck and savor until he climaxed down the back of her throat, made her core clench.

"What number is it?"

She looked up from his crotch and came into immediate eye contact with a frowning, jaw-clenching Dean. *Busted.* Her mouth dried as his gaze narrowed, piercing her with disapproval.

She glanced away, occupying herself with a frantic search

for her keys in the bottom of her handbag. The hypocritical action hadn't been lost on her either. At least she felt remorse, unlike the bartender... Well, okay, she wasn't entirely remorseful, but she never claimed to be a saint.

"Are we here already?" Her voice was too chipper as she searched her bag, pretending she hadn't been caught visually violating him.

"Yes." His answer contained an aggressive undertone.

She wasn't sure if the hostility came from having to drive her home, or because of her visual transgression.

"It's number nineteen. The one with the white mailbox."

She clasped her keys, but continued to keep her sight diverted. If she glanced between his legs one more time, she would giggle like a child.

She had to focus her attention on the quiet tree-lined street, the girls playing hopscotch on the footpath, the boys tackling each other in a game of soccer, instead of the tower of temptation in her periphery.

Or maybe talking to fill the void would be better. She should invite him inside and forget about the humiliating compliment she made about his drool-worthy aftershave.

Only problem was, the "wanna come in for coffee?" line would be asking for trouble. Especially when she didn't understand the innuendo behind the invitation.

Why wasn't a coffee, just a coffee? Why were there strings involved when said coffee was offered during flirtatious situations? Coffee deserved more respect than that. Right?

Her thoughts sharpened, giving her the clarity to realize any innuendo would be a bad idea. But she didn't want Dean to dump her and speed off into the fast approaching night. Leaving their interaction at this awkward pinnacle would make Monday morning an awaiting disaster

And besides, she wanted to stare at him a little longer. To give her drunken, slightly uninhibited self free rein to ogle, instead of ignoring her feelings like her prim and proper side insisted.

"Nice digs."

Her heart fluttered at the compliment. Some people spent their time and money on children, pets, or hobbies. She gave all she had to her townhouse.

Originally, the inside space had seemed too big for someone living alone, but her parents and out of town friends used the extra space when they traveled long distances to visit. It also helped that she didn't have an interest in going clubbing and drinking every weekend, preferring to spend her money on renovations.

Her home was her sanctuary, the place she felt safe and secure since moving to Melbourne. Each room had been decorated to suit her personality, from the feature walls to the furniture. Hours upon hours of hard work had gone into making the front yard a manicured masterpiece. So, it meant a lot to hear someone compliment her tiny piece of the world.

"Do you want to come in?" The question came out too quick. Way too quick. But hey, at least she hadn't mentioned coffee.

He continued to stare straight ahead. At her home. "I'll make sure you get settled inside. Then I need to head back to the office and finish up a few things."

The reminder hit her with another barrage of scandalous images of Max in expensive, old-man underwear, the pictures firmly nailing themselves onto the walls of her mind.

Grabbing her handbag, she climbed out of the car with intoxicated grace and navigated the few steps to her front door with more finesse than her walk through the city streets. Dean followed right behind her, silently standing by while she unlocked the door and forged inside.

His proximity made her tingle—her skin, her tongue, her nipples. She fell down a rabbit hole of sexual possibilities and lost all hope of focus. At least until she was halfway down the hall. That's when commonsense kicked in, and she stopped abruptly, turned, and slammed directly into Dean's chest.

The air left her lungs, her vision shorting for the briefest of moments as she started to fall backward. Before her ass hit the floor, his arms engulfed her, pulling her to her feet and into his arms.

"You okay?" He frowned at her, searching her eyes for an answer she was too breathless to give.

She couldn't get away from him this evening. Divine intervention seemed to be playing a part in trying to bring them together.

Not that she minded. However, she was a little disappointed her memories of his body hadn't done him justice. All those nights fantasizing of smooth skin, strong hands, and intoxicating scents didn't include a fraction of the appeal she currently rubbed against.

He was all hard, hot, and radiating testosterone, forcing her rapidly beating heart into meltdown.

"I left the keys in the front door," she admitted, her cheeks heating.

His gaze cut into her, dark and full of cocky satisfaction as he jiggled the keys from his hand wrapped behind her back.

She wanted to wipe that look off his face. To turn his smug superiority into something less intimidating. No, she *needed* to.

Before she could talk herself out of it, she pushed up on the tips of her toes and placed her mouth against his.

The connection ignited memories and fantasies like gasoline doused kindling. Lust hit her in a rush and she sank into the strength of the arms tightening around her.

She flattened her hands on the hard mounds of his pecs and fought the urge to dig her fingernails into his flesh. Restraint was key… Or it would've been.

Hell, she didn't know what the game plan was anymore.

All she could do was savor every scorching, heart-palpitating movement of their kiss and let herself be consumed by the pleasure of contentment. It was perfect. The delicate caress, the unity of chest against chest, the nervous way her belly flipped and tumbled…for all of about thirty seconds before his arms fell and he stepped back.

Total. Buzz. Kill.

A crease marred his brow as he raked a hand through his hair. "Beth." His tone held authority, even the slightest hint of a chastisement. "I'm sorry, but—"

"Don't." She threw up a hand and stepped away, frustrated at her stupidity. She didn't need him to be the voice of reason or to point out her idiocy.

She couldn't believe she'd been mindless enough to throw herself at the one man she vowed never to become involved with.

And he rejected her.

*Jackass.*

"*I'm* the one that's sorry," she added. "That was stupid of me." She continued down the hall, shame shadowing her every inch of the way. "You can let yourself out."

It took a few more steps in full-blown tipsy-tantrum mode before her mind caught up. "Oh, wait." She swung back to face him. "I need my keys."

The bastard grinned at her. The same devilish grin he used when playfully making fun of her at work.

It didn't take more than two brain cells to realize he was mentally laughing his ass off.

"You know, I've never seen you this drunk before." His mouth twitched. "I kinda like it."

"You kinda like it?" Annoyance coated her words as she planted her hands on her hips. "Yeah, you like it enough to have an erection the whole ride home, but not enough to kiss me back."

*Whoa, little lady.*

Where the hell was this humiliation fuel coming from?

She just used the word erection in front of Dean Sutherland.

*The* Dean Sutherland.

Her *boss.*

Monday was going to be one mother of a bitch.

Her throat burned in a mix of embarrassment and anger. She was overreacting. They both knew it. Too bad she couldn't stop herself. The way he stood, with his chin arrogantly high and the smug taunting smile, ate away at her, poking her closer toward the cliff's edge.

"It's okay though," she drawled. "It's selfish to expect more than one impressive Sutherland man to desire me, and your dad already voiced his interest earlier."

Silence descended like a bomb as Dean's face hardened, that cocky grin transforming into one flat line of lips.

She'd gone too far. Not only had she stepped on the imaginary line, she'd jumped over it, never to return.

Blood drained from her head with every passing second that his features hardened.

His gaze narrowed to spiteful slits. His nostrils flared. His jaw ticked.

She couldn't work out why she was being emotional and immature. This wasn't like her at all. It was pathetic and beneath her.

She swallowed over the lump in her throat and fled down the hall. Too scared to face the heat. "Please, just leave the keys on the floor on your way out."

Tears stung her eyes. Pathetic tears which had a lot to do

with sleep deprivation, stress, and the ever-annoying amount of alcohol.

It had nothing to do with his rejection.

Nothing whatsoever.

She stalked into the living room, placed her handbag on the nearest recliner, and leaned against it as she removed her shoes. She undid the straps and listened for the sound of the door, praying he would leave before her emotional breakdown took over.

"*Beth.*" His menacing voice reverberated down the hall, followed by loud approaching footfalls.

In seconds he was behind her, his presence looming close. "What the fuck does that mean?"

The anger emanating off him made her want to run. Hide. Instead, she stood her ground and tilted her chin in defiance as she turned to face him.

"You're sleeping with my father?" he growled.

She jerked back with a gasp, not only at his unrestrained vehemence, but the not-so-subtle hint of jealousy.

Two minutes ago he hadn't been interested in her at all.

"That's none of your business." She made to move around him, only to have him step in her way, hovering close.

"Like hell it's not." Pain filled the dark depths of his eyes as he leaned close, almost nose to nose. "I've waited patiently for over a year to get you back. A fucking year, Beth, and now, when you're too damn drunk and too damn emotional to think straight, you finally decide you want something from me? What's going on? And what does all this have to do with my father?"

A rush of air left her lungs.

He wanted her?

He'd been waiting?

She blinked back at him, in disbelief. And hope. And confusion.

"Are you sleeping with him?" Defeat etched his words and settled in his eyes.

"No." She shook her head to reiterate. It seemed absurd to be asked such a laughable question, but he was serious. His eyes searched hers, peering into her soul for confirmation. "I'm not sleeping with him. I never would."

"But he propositioned you."

The words hadn't been a question. He knew.

She answered anyway, needing to soothe his blatant frustration. "Yes. That's what the meeting was about this afternoon."

His thoughts were almost visible, from the darkness that curled his lip, to the fear furrowing his brow.

"You're mine," he stated with confidence, then defied the statement by retreating a step and placing more space between them.

He began to pace the living room, back and forth, over and over, his frustration not dwindling.

She didn't know what to do. What to say.

Suddenly, Monday morning seemed so much better when there had only been a kiss to contend with and the separate issue with his father. Now both problems were firmly interlocked and the approach of the new working week gathered steam like a building apocalypse.

"I need to go." He stopped before her, one hand rubbing the back of his neck, the other thrusting the keys toward her.

"Right," she whispered, entirely confused.

Over time she'd determined the relationship between Dean and his father wasn't rock solid. They dealt with each other in a sterile, professional manner and, although they rarely argued, she'd never seen them bond like father and son should. But the last thing she wanted was to become involved in a family feud.

It was also on the tip of her tongue to ask why he said the

things he did, the words that made her heart thrum and her belly flutter, but the possible repercussions weren't worth the probable boost to her ego.

She couldn't afford to have a messy relationship with him. Ignoring the entire afternoon and forgetting it happened would be best.

"Thanks for the ride home." She started for the kitchen and grabbed a bottle of water and aspirin to ward off the inevitable hangover.

It may not be completely dark yet, but the dwindling alcohol buzz and the emotional backlash had drained her. She needed to sleep…or pass out, whichever came first; whichever killed the embarrassment quicker. "I'm going to bed. Please lock up on your way out."

"We're not finished." He followed her into the kitchen. "Now you've made the first move, I won't let you back down. When you're sober and thinking straight, I'll be here. I'm not letting you walk away again."

She paused, a halfhearted chuckle leaving her lips before she headed for the stairs leading to the second floor and her bedroom. "Whatever you say, Dean."

"Scoff all you like, but mark my words, I'm not backing down."

Tingles of hope ran up the back of her neck. Her heart was already convinced, screaming for her to turn, to run to him and find what she craved in his arms. But she couldn't.

Month after month, week after week, she had listened to the office gossip of the nameless, faceless women who shared his bed, each woman lasting a few nights of passion before he moved on.

He was a player—a man incapable of commitment—and although she wanted to believe there was more to him, to convince herself this infatuation wasn't a mere physical attraction, she knew better. Men were creatures of habit.

They couldn't go from eating a smorgasbord of top quality delicacies, day in, day out, to a set diet for the rest of their lives.

He obviously loved his...menu.

Her life, on the other hand, was stable. Predictable. She needed to maintain that equilibrium. He was only trying to lighten an uncomfortable situation, using his charm to make her feel better about herself.

He didn't truly like her, not the way she wanted, the way she needed. He was an unrepentant womanizer, and she was looking for a future.

"I'll believe it when I see it," she whispered.

# CHAPTER 4

*B*eth woke to an alarming case of alcohol-induced embarrassment. Add a mild headache, a severe taste of gravel mouth, and she hoped the day could only get better.

*Please, God, let it get better.*

She sank further under the covers and groaned at the overwhelming memories of Dean. In less than an hour, she'd completely messed up their friendship and professional relationship. But at least she'd achieved it in her typical efficient manner, right?

She cringed at the thought of how badly his opinion of her would have changed. He probably labelled her desperate for trying to kiss him. Or childish for the way she reacted to his rejection.

No doubt he thought she was bat shit crazy, too, for mentioning his father's proposition.

She wallowed, holding the sheet over her head for long, suffocating minutes. There was no point worrying about something she couldn't change. But achieving that feat was easier said than done.

She needed to deal with the brain fade in a calm and professional manner—exactly the opposite of how she'd handled yesterday. Only the thought of seeing him again made her stomach roil.

"Give me strength." She threw back the covers and blinked the sleep from her eyes.

Her room was still in darkness and the fuzzy red numbers on the bedside clock made her groan. It wasn't even six o'clock yet. Waking before sunrise on a weekend was sacrilegious, even when it was karma's subtle way of giving her a kick in the ass.

She rolled from the bed, blindly walking to her bathroom, hoping a long, steamy shower would wash away the niggling headache and self-pity.

Fifteen minutes later, she was shampooed and smelling like an overripe strawberry. She'd even found a positive spin on the situation under the shower's relaxing spray.

Dean wouldn't hold a grudge.

He loved to tease and embarrass, and if goading remarks were the worst of her worries, it wouldn't be the end of the world. They could move forward, remain friends, and she would continue to lust after him from a distance, praying her resistance didn't wear down for a third time.

First thing Monday morning, she planned on apologizing.

She would brush off the kiss, claim it was nothing more than drunken stupidity, and move on with her life. Hell, she would even bite her tongue and let Dean enjoy the teasing torture she knew he would inflict, over and over and over again.

She could deal with it.

What she couldn't deal with right now were thoughts of his father and the nightmare of a proposition. How would she let her boss down gently without risking her job?

The search for the illusive answer made her hangover symptoms increase.

Using a plush towel, she dried the excess moisture from her hair, wrapped the heavy material around her body, and secured it above her breasts. As she raised her gaze to the mirror, she bit her lip and smiled at the memory of Dean's mouth on hers. It may have been a mistake—a monumental one—but it had been the most wickedly delicious mistake.

At least when the embarrassment at work became too much, she could gain solace from the images she would never allow to dissipate from her mind.

Soft, dominant lips.

Strong, unyielding arms.

Firm muscled pecs, and a scent sinful enough to intoxicate the gods.

Only time would tell if those delicious memories would be worth the backlash. The images also left a heavy ache in her chest. Despite her rational mind knowing Dean wasn't the one, her heart and body believed otherwise.

She had to remind herself he wasn't the type to settle for a white picket fence and 2.5 children. He liked fast women. The ones who sped in and out of his bedroom. The types who didn't want a romantic future or commitment.

She pasted on a bright smile, hoping a cheerful expression would be enough to initiate a similar emotion. It didn't work. Her chest throbbed, her eyes glazed, and she had to glance away, unable to stand her own pathetic longing.

Dean wasn't the one for her. She knew that. The sooner her heart caught up to speed, the better.

With a sigh, she flicked off the bathroom light and walked into her bedroom in search of clothes. She couldn't see a damn thing in the darkness, only a dawning sense of unease accompanied her across the room.

Her skin prickled. The hair on the back of her neck stood on end.

Something wasn't right.

She froze and did a slow visual sweep of her surroundings to determine the cause of her unsettled nerves while her eyes gradually adapted.

Everything seemed as it should be. The curtains were still closed with the first rays of sun breaching the edges. The bed was a mess of tangled sheets, just the way she'd left it. No furniture stood out of place. The clothes she threw off last night still lay haphazardly on the floor. But her skin still crawled with ominous awareness.

Did Dean forget to lock her front door when he left yesterday?

She took another step as a squeak of noise sounded from the hallway. Her heart exploded with erratic beats, the pulse pounding all the way up her throat.

Someone was in her house.

She scrutinized the doorway, staring with intent as the blackness turned to shades of gray. Her sight began to focus and a dark figure appeared.

Someone was there.

In her doorway.

She didn't pause to contemplate an escape plan. She opened her mouth and let loose with a piercing scream. The noise stung her ears but didn't smother the muttered curse coming from the doorway.

She rushed for the bedside lamp and flicked it on. The brilliant burst of yellow temporarily blinded her, cutting off her scream as she snapped her eyes shut. She threw up her arms in a lame attempt to protect herself and stepped back, blinking wildly.

"Calm down," the man demanded.

With each blink her sight adjusted and the familiar masculine frame came into view. "Dean?"

He leaned against the door frame in the same clothes from the day before, sans shoes and socks. His hair stood on end as if ruffled from sleep while those wicked eyes raked over her, head to foot. A grin pulled at his lips while he inspected her. A damn grin bright enough to light a stadium.

She measured her breathing, trying to slow her heart rate, and lowered her arm to her side. Her wrist brushed the softness of the towel and her mouth gaped as she realized she stood before him half-naked, hair dripping.

*Oh, shit.*

She swung her hands to her chest, frantically reaching for the top of the towel to ensure her important bits were covered.

His smile only widened, his eyes twinkling in barely contained humor.

"What the hell are you still doing here?" The question came out in a breathy rasp, all feminine and meek.

His focus intensified, gliding over her skin like a caress, the visual touch made her nipples tighten and tingle. He pushed from the door frame and took the first step toward her. "Like I said last night, I'm done waiting."

---

He stared at the vision before him, his heart melting. He'd anticipated this moment, had imagined it in his mind. All. Night. Long.

She had made it clear she didn't believe his declaration—*As soon as you're sober and thinking straight I'll be here.*

In all honesty, he hadn't meant the words literally. His

intention had been to discuss their situation in a few days, a few weeks at most, when things settled.

He'd wanted to change his approach. He'd been treading lightly since their last disastrous kiss, trying to get the relationship back to the way it was previously. His flirting had been subtle, his intent less obvious, while he waited for their friendship to lose the edge of discomfort.

But it wasn't until she scoffed last night, showing a complete lack of faith, that the determination to prove her wrong kicked in.

This time things would be different. Instead of giving her time, he planned on taking the no-bullshit approach. He'd decided to handle her the way he was most comfortable and confident with. Through temptation and excessive charm.

Not only would he literally seduce the pants right off her, he had no plan of giving her a few weeks to sort her shit out. He made the commitment not to give her a single day to contemplate.

So, instead of heading to the office after she stormed to bed, he waited downstairs like a psychotic stalker. He'd remained quiet until he was confident she was asleep, then he started for the stairs to her room.

It hadn't been hard to find. A skylight in the middle of the hall lit the way, and all the doors had been closed except one. He had walked closer, taking the time to appreciate the family photos hanging on the walls. Each piece acted as a minor distraction as he worked his way to the open door at the end of the hall.

When he reached her room, his breath caught. The light of the setting sun peeked over the curtains, bathing her in a soft glow. She had been entirely peaceful. No stress from work tightened her features. No flirty smile. Just calm, fragile beauty.

His heart had hammered while he stood silently watching

her sleep. Her hair splayed across the pillow, the pink feminine pajamas leaving little to the imagination as her bare legs straddled the cream silk sheets.

Her barely audible whimpers made his dick pulse. He fantasized about those feminine sounds escaping her lips for completely different reasons.

Dirty reasons.

Filthy reasons.

His vision blurred with the images of naked, entangled limbs until the need to glide his fingers over her curves became a consuming ache.

With a shake of his head, he had retreated downstairs. He chose to spend the night on her couch, less than impressed with his cock that felt the need to point at the roof for hours on end.

He couldn't quit thinking about her—running his tongue along the delicate skin at the low of her back, how he would devour her mouth with heated kisses, the way he would savor her mewls and screams as he made her come with his fingers, his tongue, his cock.

He would make love to her, hot and heavy, soft and sweet, long and languid, however she wanted—all day, until she quit questioning his motives.

Every minute of that long-ass night had been torture. An unrelenting fight with temptation. The only thing that stopped him walking back upstairs to part her silken thighs had been his need to plot a plan of attack.

By the time early morning arrived he was delirious from lack of sleep, and convinced he had visualized having sex with her in every fucking way imaginable.

The Kama Sutra of Beth had engrained itself into every square inch of his mind.

Every. Square. Inch.

The sound of the running water from the upstairs bathroom had been a welcomed reprieve from the sexual delirium. She was awake, and although he couldn't remember having slept, he felt alert, ready to run a marathon like the damn Energizer Bunny.

Now she stood before him in nothing but a towel. Her skin glistened with moisture, her hair was dark and heavy over her exposed shoulders. She clung to the purple material like a lifeline and he wondered if he'd made a mistake in staying over.

He'd had good intentions. At least they had seemed that way from his perspective. What worried him the most was her expression, a look he tried to convince himself was merely shock, not utter terror.

"What do you mean you're done waiting?" Her voice trembled the slightest bit.

For a second he couldn't even remember what he meant either. His mind had become fixated on her creamy skin and the way the short towel made her legs appear ten miles long.

"I told you yesterday that when you were sober and thinking straight, I'd be here."

Her mouth fell open, then snapped shut, pausing a moment before it opened again. "Y-you don't have to do this."

She backed away and he had to admit he liked her discomfort. She always had an air of peaceful serenity at work, only ever showing emotion if he held her gaze a little too long, or flirted a little too much. It felt damn good to have her flustered for once.

"To make me feel better, I mean," she continued. "I know throwing myself at you was embarrassing, but it was a stupid drunken moment that we both need to forget."

Okay, so she wasn't groveling at his feet just yet. No biggie.

He hadn't expected her to drop the towel, sashay her sexy

ass over, and get on her knees…although it had been among a shitload of fantasies he enjoyed during the early hours.

She had more class. She wasn't a seductress, and even though she initiated the kiss yesterday, it never would've happened without the alcoholic confidence.

Her unease didn't ruin his plan. He could make do with her being flustered and apprehensive.

He took a step forward, approaching with his heart hammering behind tightening ribs. Her eyes widened and her hand clutched tighter on the towel.

He was close enough to reach out and touch her, to move his hands over the delicate lines of her collarbone and wipe the loose strands of damp hair away from her face. But he didn't. Instead, he focused on the way her teeth bit into her bottom lip, the plump, crimson flesh calling to him like a beacon.

"I don't regret what happened for a second." He should have wooed her, laying on a thick speech about his feelings and all that soft, sweet stuff.

She deserved a man who could give her the words to back up the emotion. But that wasn't him. He could only comprehend telling her how much he craved her like a drug. How her beauty surpassed comprehension. Or that her smile was the first thing he thought of whenever he woke up. "I've wanted you for so damn long."

She had to know her sexy mouth drove him to madness. Watching her teeth dig into that sultry lower lip made him wild.

She retreated another step, bumping into the bedside table. Her eyes never left his while she righted herself, as if he were a predatory animal about to pounce.

Maybe he was.

"We can't do this. You're my boss, and your dad…" She cringed, glancing away momentarily before dragging her gaze back with focused determination. "We just can't do this, okay?"

Her words held conviction, but her eyes lacked the sentiment. She wanted this. Wanted him. She was only worried about the possible ramifications.

Case in point—her gaze dipped to his mouth, her tongue poking out to moisten her lips.

His resistance shot straight to hell. He closed the distance between them with one step and leaned his face into hers. He inhaled her gasp of surprise and took her mouth with his, strong and determined.

The heat of her skin sank into him, rushing through his veins like liquid fire and shooting straight to his cock.

He'd had the pleasure of experiencing her kiss twice, both times blowing his mind. Yet, they didn't compare to this pleasure or intensity.

Before, there had been doubts and second-guessing. Now, there would be no backing down.

He gripped her arms, holding her steady. He continued to kiss and lick and suck at her lips, expecting resistance. She gave him none, opening her mouth to him, succumbing.

His tongue coaxed hers in soft strokes of appreciation as he moved one hand up her arm, over her shoulder, around her nape. He threaded his fingers through her damp hair, his other arm trailing around to encase her waist. He pulled her close, thigh to thigh, pelvis to pelvis. The lightest friction of her body against his drew a moan from his throat, his hunger all the more palpable as he devoured her.

She still gripped the towel, her hand confirming her reluctance to surrender completely. But her body softened and the tentative glide of her tongue increased.

Gradually, she molded into him, one hand timidly climbing up his stomach, the simple touch enough to make his cock jerk.

He lowered his arm from her waist, sending his hand on a path to firmly grasp her ass. He ground into her, their tongues tangling, hips rocking.

He fought to remain in control as her needy whimper jolted his senses, the feminine sound drifting from her lips and into his mouth. He couldn't get enough of her—the way her fingernails dug into his skin, the sweet, fruity smell of her, or how her tongue sparred with his in an erotic dance.

She was perfect.

Responsive.

Greedy.

Heavenly.

He needed to have her. To take her to bed and concentrate on nothing except their lust until they were sated and sore.

But no matter how much her touch consumed him, or her growing hunger demanded his attention, a thought still niggled at the back of his mind, pissing him the fuck off.

His father wanted her.

God. Damn. It.

What perfect timing to think of his dear old dad. No way in hell would he allow his father's hands anywhere near her. She belonged right where she was and he would do whatever necessary to make his father realize that.

Not that this was the first time a proposition had been made to someone Dean cared about. The last time had come seven years ago when Max had unforgivably stolen the woman Dean had been sleeping with.

*No,* he'd been falling in love with her.

His father's words still rang in his ears—*a woman willing to take money to sleep with another man isn't someone you want to waste your time on, son.*

The heat increased in his veins, turning his desire into a challenge to win.

Couldn't the old bastard see Beth was different?

She was too innocent, too sweet, too much of a kind-hearted woman under all that sassy exterior.

There was no way in hell he would let his father touch her, let alone fuck her.

No. Way. In. Hell.

He pulled back, breaking the kiss to rest his forehead against hers. They stood in silence, their chests heaving, their breath mingling.

She glanced at him with wide eyes, her fingers clinging to his shirt as if she would crumple to the floor without the tight grasp.

Nothing would take this away from him. He refused to let anything come between them again. Not work. Not his pride. And definitely not his family.

She had been his since their first kiss. She knew it. He knew it. His father probably knew it, too, which would explain the conniving proposition.

There was no turning back this time.

He gripped her chin and spoke against her lips. "I won't let him have you."

ean's words were a cold dose of reality.

When he first entered her room, he'd sent her reeling, making it a struggle not to drown in arousal.

Now she didn't know what to think. It sounded like he was trying to prove a point. To win a challenge against his father that he didn't need to compete in. Surely, he couldn't be that cruel.

Before she could open her mouth to question his motives, he moved his hands, sliding them over her shoulders and down to grip her ass.

Her concentration disappeared and the tingling his touch inspired overtook her unease.

His mouth lowered to hers again, lips plundering, tongue more demanding, and the inner muscles of her thighs tightened in response. He ground into her, the hard length of him still clearly felt through his clothes and her towel.

He lifted her, the hands on her ass sliding lower to guide her thighs around his waist while they kissed. She locked her ankles around his butt and clung to him.

The towel started to stretch, creeping up her legs until

her most intimate flesh became exposed. Her cheeks heated, the warmth descending from her neck to pool in her chest.

She needed to yank the material down, to cover herself, and in equal measure she didn't want to draw attention and show her sexual shyness.

She wasn't a virgin by any means, but her lovers had been few and far between. And if she compared herself to Dean, her tally would be closer to the Virgin Mary's.

The reminder of her inexperience made it hard to concentrate. Their teeth collided, over and over. Their tongues quit moving in a choreographed rhythm. Their kiss became a mass of fumbling movements.

"You okay?" He leaned back, his eyes reading her with concern as she willed him to keep eye contact.

*Please, do not look down.*

"Yes." She gave him a jerky nod.

He paused, scrutinizing her before he tilted his face again, moving in for another kiss. She let out a barely audible sigh as he moved closer, their lips almost brushing. But he didn't bridge the distance. Instead, his head continued to slant into hers, his gaze drifting lower, down her body to take in her spread sex.

The lustful rumble that emanated from his chest sent the fire burning between her legs into overdrive, equal parts lust and mortification. She lifted his chin with a delicate finger, guiding his sight back to hers. His gaze was animalistic, primitive as she leaned in to distract him, planting a slow kiss on his lips.

"Beth." Her name was a plea. A whisper of longing that filled her with the slightest dose of strength.

She enjoyed his torment. Absolutely loved his desire. His lust gave her the confidence to shamelessly run her tongue along his lip, nipping it with her teeth until his moan echoed through her.

He turned, walking them toward the bed to lay her down on the tangled covers. Her towel held firm around her breasts, but the bottom splayed open, leaving her pussy exposed.

On shaky elbows she leaned up and watched Dean's eyes brazenly devour her. His nostrils flared, his jaw tightened. He was enraptured. By *her*.

His intensity empowered her, giving her the confidence to let him feast a little longer.

"Christ, you're mesmerizing." The huskiness of his voice sent a shiver over her skin and her heart slammed into her throat. "I could stare at you like this for hours."

She smiled at his compliment, but self-consciousness made it impossible to keep her legs parted. She closed her thighs, obstructing his view and allowing the insecurity to return.

He shook his head, clucking his tongue in disapproval. "Keep them open."

She whimpered at the command, completely powerless to the way he made her feel gorgeous with only a few words, a few steamy touches, and a wicked gleam in his eye.

She dropped back on the bed and had to drape an arm over her eyes while he blatantly admired her wet and throbbing sex.

He knelt between her legs and her core clenched in response. Slowly, he spread her further and further, wider and wider, until her pulse pounded in her ears and her skin beaded with sweat.

She could sense his gaze, could almost feel it on her heated skin.

The brush of his lips scorched her knee, his lips burning a trail along her inner thighs. Soft kisses turned to teasing nips while his hands slid down her calves to grip her ankles. He guided her legs over his shoulder, skyrocketing her apprehension and arousal.

His ascent was torture. The licking. The nuzzling. All the way to her core.

Then he stopped.

He didn't move. Didn't speak.

She dropped her arm from her eyes, waiting, wondering what he would do next.

His gaze met hers as he hovered his mouth an inch away from her opening. His heavy breathing ran over her, each exhalation touching her like a finger through her folds.

She squirmed, needing penetration.

Needing something.

Anything.

He maintained eye contact as his tongue flicked out, taking a long, ruthless swipe of her heat.

Pleasure shot through her. The tingles and wildfire burning nerves and skin and organs.

He moved closer, delved deeper. First one stroke, then two. Each lash of his tongue became harder, faster, more demanding, making the need to grind her thighs together unbearable.

"*Dean.*" Her voice filled with raw hunger. She was falling apart and soaring on a high, needing more, yet not wanting it to end.

He trailed a hand over her waist, to the edge of the towel and gave a firm yank.

She gasped, his movement pulling her forward, sending his tongue drilling into her slick channel while the towel loosened and fell to her sides.

She leaned up on shaky elbows and watched the delicate exploration of his fingers. His hand slid over her belly, caressing her ribs, teasing the underside of her breast before cupping and firmly grasping.

He was relentless, his hand kneading, squeezing, and lightly pinching. His mouth found her clit—sucking, blowing —until pleasure had her back arched off the bed.

Her body was in agonizing bliss, caught between the need for climax and the greed for this euphoria to continue.

She wanted more, wanted everything, and wanted it only from this man.

"Let go for me." His other hand found her heat, trailing light strokes up and down, up and down before breeching her slit.

The hand on her breast, the mouth on her clit, the fingers in her pussy… It all became too much.

She fell, plummeting over the edge, losing herself to ecstasy. Pleasure wracked her body, consuming every pore. She grasped the hand at her breast and clenched her thighs. Greedy, so greedy for more.

And still his mouth continued to devour, his fingers penetrating, his hand squeezing. She closed her eyes, shamelessly grinding into him, over and over, until the spasms faded and reality seeped in.

Dean's hands, mouth, and heat abandoned her at the same time, and she couldn't bring herself to open her eyes. Doubt and fear clawed their way into her mind.

What would happen on Monday?

How would he act after this?

She closed her legs and turned them to the side in a vain attempt to hide. Then she increased her cowardice by placing her hands over her face to ward off the shame and stupidity.

She had been strong for so long, resisting his charms. Then in one moment of weakness, all her hard work had burned to ash. She couldn't stand the thought of opening her eyes and seeing his smirk of satisfaction.

And the whiplash… It was remarkable. One minute her love life had been nonexistent; the next she was mistress material, and in a blink of an eye she was shamelessly grinding against Dean's face.

His handsome, talented face.

*Jesus Christ.*

No wonder women flocked to him.

His cockiness was clearly justified.

The grate of a zipper startled her from her internal tirade. She dropped her hands from her face and clutched to find the towel to sit against on the edge of the mattress.

He stood at her feet, bare-chested and on display for her greedy gaze to devour, his fingers still gripping his lowered zipper.

She wanted to moan at the perfection, at the sun-darkened skin, the strong frame, and the light trail of hair traveling down from his navel.

He lowered his pants, displaying the erection jutting from the top of his gray boxer briefs. She kept her sight centered on the juncture of his thighs, prolonging the fantasy as long as she could, unable to meet the arrogance she expected to see on his face.

Her heart thundered as he shoved his trousers below his ass, down a damn fine pair of tanned, muscular legs before they fell in a heap on the floor.

Her eyes feasted, taking in the dips and curves, the hardness, the beauty.

A glint of silver in his hand caught her attention and held. He grasped a foil packet, and the end result to his striptease finally cemented in her mind.

Her throat dried as she raised her gaze. She expected to see smug satisfaction, at least a hint of arrogance.

What she found was entirely different. There was no cocky grin, no gleam in his eye, no heated smile. He stood there, emotionally bare, his face a mix of undeniable lust and insecurity.

"Dean, I…"

Can't?

Shouldn't?

Her mind volunteered responses that wouldn't move past her throat. She was a mess, not only mesmerized by his body but by his vulnerable expression.

The playboy was still there, threateningly close in his confident stance, yet his eyes held a glimmer of the same fragility filling her chest. He remained silent, his gaze unwavering as he cocked a brow in question.

When no words came, he moved forward, his determination masking the uncertainty. He nudged her feet apart with his knee, his straining boxers begging to be touched.

"You what?" he murmured. "You want my mouth back on your sweet pussy? You want me inside you? You want me to make you scream again?"

Scream?

*Again?*

Her pulse raced with their contrasting opinions of how this interlude would end. She needed to tell him to leave, even after what they had shared. She needed to make him understand their working relationship wouldn't stand a chance if sex became involved.

It was better, for them both, if they simply pretended this never happened.

His fingers reached out, trailing along her jaw, under her chin, to lift until she peered into his eyes.

He shook his head. "I've wanted to be here for a long time. In your house. In your bed." His thumb caressed her bottom lip. "I can tell what you're thinking, and you're wrong. This isn't a mistake."

He leaned down, kissing her, soft and slow and sweet. She could taste her arousal on his lips, and smell the musky scent on his skin. It was all too much. The surplus pleasure. The glut of lust.

"We're good together. You know we are." His words became a whisper as he continued to kiss her with delicate splendor, decimating her doubt and making her yearn for more. "You can feel it just as much as I can."

He was right. She *could* feel it. But that didn't mean what they were doing was appropriate.

Regret would hound them in the aftermath. So much regret.

And still she couldn't back away when his mouth pressed harder, his tongue moving in an adamant glide against hers. She released her grip on the towel with a tiny mewl of capitulation.

Continuing was a mistake, yet the need flowing through her veins wouldn't allow her to stop.

He shucked his boxer briefs without parting their lips, his hasty movements adding to the urgency. She maneuvered onto her knees, gliding her fingers into his hair, holding him close while she scooted back on the bed.

He followed, making the mattress dip from his weight. With strong hands he gripped her hips, pivoting her to place her back against the pillows.

Their teeth clanged on the descent, his hard chest pressing into her.

As their teeth and tongues clashed, he encouraged her to spread her thighs, and then knelt between them.

He broke the kiss and planted soft pecks on her lips before pulling back to rest on his haunches. He looked deep into her eyes and tore the condom wrapper with his teeth.

Her focus followed his hands, the way he firmly grasped his cock and started covering his length.

Her throat went dry at the sight of him, thick and long. His erection was larger than she anticipated, standing proud from the nest of dark curls at the base of his shaft. She couldn't deny her apprehension over his size, but her skin also tingled in excitement knowing he would soon be inside her.

She swallowed, trying to contain herself, hoping her adrenaline would die down so her heart would slow its incessant pounding. Then he grinned at her, his eyes glowing with enthusiasm, and her heart had no chance of recovering.

"Tell me you want this." The strength of his tone wavered, betraying the confidence he tried to exude.

She swallowed the lump in her throat and nodded. She *did* want this. She just didn't want to think of the consequences.

When he moved on top of her, positioning his hard length against her, her whole body shuddered. With a deep breath she let go of her conscience. There would be time to wallow later.

Her toes curled and her nipples tingled with impatient desire as she tried not to beg to be taken. His mouth found her neck, his teeth scraping the erogenous zone at the juncture of her shoulder.

She nuzzled into him, nipping his earlobe, taking it into her mouth as she arched her back. He continued to torment her, his hand finding her breast while he took over teasing her entrance with his shaft. Lightly pushing and retreating, pushing and retreating until she couldn't take it anymore.

Running her hands up his back to his shoulders, she sank her nails in, delighting at the hiss of breath against her skin and the deeper thrust of his hardness.

He responded by nibbling her neck, the mix of pleasure and pain causing her to whimper. "Tell me you want this."

She moaned her response, wanting to scream in ecstasy when the thick head of him penetrated her, stopping just inside her opening. Wrapping her legs around his hips, she lifted her ass, trying to find the penetration her body craved, needing him deeper.

He wouldn't allow it.

"Tell me." His voice taunted her. He pulled back to lean on one elbow, their stomachs no longer touching.

Unable to deny him, to deny herself, she whimpered, "Yes."

She arched her back, her body thrumming, trying to regain the heavenly friction. He continued to caress her breast, squeezing her nipple.

She couldn't help pleading, "Yes, I want this. I want this so much."

The full weight of his body moved over her, his mouth eagerly claiming hers while he nudged her entrance. Then with one deep stroke, he plunged inside.

The air left her lungs, and he replied with a savage groan. He began to thrust, a slow, delicious onslaught that had her nails sinking deeper into his skin.

She floated in a dreamy state of reality. The man she lusted after, the one she wanted more than anyone was in her bed and making love to her.

"You're driving me crazy," he groaned. "I'm worried this won't last long."

A smile tipped her lips, and she hoped her gratitude over his ability to make her confident in this situation was evident on her face. No other man had made her feel this feminine and wanton. The sense of empowerment made her giddy, demanding her to push the limits of his control.

Deliberately clamping her muscles down on him, squeezing his hardness tighter, she relished his moan. Adored the way his whole body tensed while her thighs gripped his waist.

"Ahh, Beth." He paused his thrusts. "You're killing me."

Dying to give them both release, she gyrated her hips, the

sensation sending her close to the precipice. She grasped his ass in her hands and pulled him closer, wanting him deeper.

*Needing* him.

He obeyed, answering her unspoken command by driving into her, filling her completely before retreating and doing it again.

His thrusts increased in pace, in strength, in urgency. Their bodies shone with sweat. He pinched one of her nipples, the bite of pain ripping a scream from her lungs. The orgasm took over her body, making her core pulse in incessant fury. Her vision splintered as he continued to make love to her, each thrust adding to her pleasure until moments later he yelled his own release.

He smothered butterfly kisses along her jaw, her neck, her shoulder as his movements slowed, then stopped. With her eyes still closed she released a contented sigh and measured her breathing, inhaling the new scent of Dean and sweat and sex.

She lay boneless and sated, practically purring in contentment. She had always enjoyed sex, the intimacy and pleasure that a lover could provide, but what they just shared had been an entirely different experience.

Wow. Just wow.

When he rolled off her and then the bed, she opened her eyes and caught a glimpse of his muscled ass as he walked to her bathroom.

What happened now?

She wasn't familiar with casual sex protocol. Would he get dressed, then leave? Should she make him coffee? Was she supposed to get dressed?

She drew the sheets over her chest, apprehension coiling in her belly while he used the basin. When he walked back into the room, she tracked his movements to the door.

To the goddamn door.

Panic ran wild in her veins.

He was deserting her already.

But instead of leaving, he flicked off the light and stalked toward the bed.

In the soft glow of the sun's early rays, she concentrated on the rigid muscles of his stomach. She wondered again if his expression would be cocky, and didn't dare look. She was sated, enjoying the deep emotions weighing down her chest. She wouldn't allow herself to ruin the fantasy.

Without acknowledging his clothes, he climbed onto the bed, lifted the sheet, and snuggled into her. His warmth touched every inch of her skin as his chin came to rest on the top of her head, his arms holding her tight so her body molded into his.

"You're amazing." He tightened his hold and placed a soft kiss on her forehead.

No, *he* was amazing. And the way he made her feel was even better.

She snuggled further into him, trying to come up with a compliment that suited her mood, but before she could find the words, his breathing changed, telling her he was no longer conscious to hear it.

# CHAPTER 6

*D*ean had a smile on his face as he stretched his arm across the bed, searching for Beth. Even dazed from sleep he still felt like he was made of awesome.

He had slept with her.

Jesus H. Christ.

He. Had. Slept. With. Her.

All the saints from all the religions wouldn't dare to throw shade on this out-of-wedlock moment it was that fucking brilliant.

But vacant warm sheets were all that greeted his fingers. No silken skin, no luscious body, just emptiness filled with her intoxicating scent. Damn. He'd planned on delving between those thighs one more time before he let her out of bed.

Opening his eyes, he sat up with a yawn and listened for an indication of where she could be. A vague babble came from downstairs, the television maybe. The sound was too soft to make out. He moved from the bed to investigate, yanked on his boxer briefs and pants, then headed down to find her. By the time he reached the bottom step, he realized the noise wasn't the damn TV.

What the hell was his father doing here?

He strode through the living room, toward the hall, and the front door. His chest began to pound, jealousy and anger stopping his momentum when he found her standing in a skimpy bathrobe that barely covered her body.

As he moved in behind her, she cut him a quick glance, her eyes wide with panic. She shooed him with her hand and mouthed for him to go away.

Fuck that.

He had to confront his father. To tell him to back off. It may make things uncomfortable for her, especially at work on Monday, but there was no way around it. His father needed to leave her alone.

Positioning himself against the wall, he pulled the door open a little wider, making sure her body remained hidden. The sight of his father made his head throb. Dressed smart as always, his suit pants and crisp shirt were without the slightest wrinkle.

His father's eyes narrowed before he tilted his head in acknowledgment. "Son."

"What are you doing here?" Dean asked without preamble, unable to hide his hostility.

Beth squeezed his arm, and he took the gesture as a plea to be civil, but after the morning they'd shared, he couldn't stand his father being anywhere near her.

Call it jealousy.

Call it juvenile.

He didn't give a shit.

He wanted the man away from her, not just now—for good. So yeah, working together would be inconvenient.

"I could ask you the same question. I noticed your car in the driveway and assumed Beth had borrowed it to get home. I had hoped you weren't foolish enough to spend the night."

Foolish enough? He raised his brows and took a deep breath through his nose, trying to keep his cool. The man could write the book on foolish decisions concerning women.

"And why would spending the night be foolish?"

His father scoffed, then continued to stare at him with a scowl. Dean knew the man was weighing his options. He wouldn't want to cause a scene in front of Beth. Oh no, Max Sutherland couldn't appear unprofessional in public.

When Dean was a child, he had been flogged with his father's belt until he couldn't walk, all because he threw a tantrum at a function with extended family. He'd been seven at the time, dying for attention from his father. Attention that never came. Not in the way he wanted.

He'd grown up believing his father didn't mind if their lives fell apart behind the scenes, as long as people weren't exposed to their dirty laundry.

"You know exactly why being here is inappropriate. You don't hide your reputation."

Dean could only blink while his head threatened to explode. He wasn't sure if the remark about his reputation was for argument's sake or to remind Beth and gain the upper hand. But his father had no right to judge. At least the women Dean slept with understood his one-night-only rule. He never misled them, never committed to anything but physical gratification.

He clenched his jaw and glared. The man had cheated on Dean's mother for years, then left her to be with a gold digger half his age. Not to mention how Max rejected his own daughter, forgetting she even existed. Yet Dean was in the wrong? His father was nothing but a hypocrite.

"So what?" Dean spat. "You're allowed to proposition her like a hooker, but I can't fuck her unless I offer her money?"

He wanted to shock and inflict pain—and he had. Only he realized too late who he'd really hurt.

Beth gasped and slipped her hand from his arm. Her wide eyes scrutinized him, as if she no longer recognized who he was.

Shit.

He always watched his tongue around Beth. Trust him to pick this most inappropriate time to be a crass bastard.

"Goddamn it, Dean." His father shook his head in disgust. "After all these years, you still haven't grown up."

The disappointment hit him with the force of a sledge-hammer, the air leaving his lungs in a huff. At thirty-two years of age he should have overcome the need to please the man he despised. "You don't even know me."

"Oh no?" Max's brows rose. "You go home every weekend with a different woman. You don't respect them. You don't care about them. You're only concerned with yourself. And you make the receptionist screen your calls, for Christ's sake." He paused, gaining composure, and turned his atten-tion to Beth. "You don't deserve his flippant attitude." He glared back at Dean. "I can't believe you would be so petty, using Beth like this to get back at me."

His father didn't elaborate, letting the words fall like stones. They both knew what he referred to, but he was wrong. This had nothing to do with Jessica, nothing to do with the past. This was about Beth, about sating a hunger he'd let eat away at him for too long. It was about taking a chance with a beautiful woman who he respected and adored.

Dean glanced away, needing to concentrate before he flipped out. Over time he hoped the wealth of hatred he held for his father would dissipate. It hadn't. He only learned to mask it better and with their issues moving back to the fore-front, the animosity began to resurface, bringing the betrayal back in raw, unyielding pain.

He remembered the events with vivid clarity. His mother's tears, her sobbing wails as her hands shook, craving the medication to take away her heartache. The misery that consumed his younger sister over losing a father who was still alive, and how Dean had to adapt to the role even though he was a child himself.

The memories of Jessica still hurt too; however, the woman herself barely rated a mention. He'd once thought he was falling in love with her. Now he knew better. When he'd caught her with his father, all cherished feelings for them both had fled.

His old man sighed and gave another shake of his head. Dean bit his tongue, pressing down until he tasted the coppery tang of blood.

"I'm sorry to cause you all this trouble, Beth," his father offered. "Please remember what I said earlier."

Dean was anxious to find out what they'd discussed but kept his mouth shut. Extending the conversation would only make this fucked-up situation worse, and he'd put her through enough already.

She gave a quick nod and remained quiet beside him. Without acknowledging Dean, his father dipped his head in farewell and walked away. Soon after, Beth did the same, turning to move with quick steps down the hall. He waited, needing to make sure his father left.

It wasn't until the black Mercedes pulled away from the curb and drove out of sight that he slammed the front door. The sound vibrated off the walls, piercing his ears, adding to the fury boiling inside him.

He wanted to yell.

He wanted to punch something.

Hell, he would settle for a stiff drink, but right now he had to fix this mess.

He stormed through the silent living room, past the kitchen, scanning each in search of her. Taking the stairs three at a time, he stalked down the hall and to her bedroom.

Apprehension tightened his chest as he approached her door. He couldn't remember the last time he'd argued with a lover—apart from Jessica—and he didn't know what to expect.

Beth had a kind heart and he couldn't imagine her lashing out, but angry women were temperamental. One minute they smiled, proclaiming nothing was wrong, the next your dick was in a blender with their finger hovering over the On switch.

He leaned on the outside of the door frame, deciding to watch her for a moment. He wasn't a chickenshit; he held back to give her space. And if that time allowed him to determine if she held any sharp objects, it would be all the better.

Tracking her movements, her body now dressed in a loose T-shirt and tiny sweat shorts, he figured the guilt stabbing under his ribs couldn't be worse than any physical pain she could inflict.

"I'm sorry." He took the first step into the room.

Her spine stiffened, and she turned her neck to peer at him over her shoulder, his shirt in her hands. Her expression didn't portray any emotion, no anger, no frustration, no betrayal. Only the faintest hint of sadness in her eyes. She masked her feelings under a cool facade and walked over to hand him the shirt without making eye contact.

"Nothing to be sorry for." She turned and busied herself making the bed. "I understand. It was just sex. I may not be known for sleeping around, but I'm not naive. I realize you're a player, and I slept with you anyway."

He cringed.

He'd never had a problem with his reputation before, but hearing the words from her lips made him feel less than worthy. He wanted to be good enough for her, someone she could be proud of. Not the sleazy womanizer the guys at work loved to congratulate.

"Beth." He stepped closer. Her eyes would tell him exactly how she felt, how bad he'd hurt her. He just needed her to lift her deliberately downcast gaze.

"Look at me." He held his breath while she turned to focus on him through dark lashes. Her chin may be high, but he took the time to notice the little things she couldn't hide. The way her throat convulsed with a swallow. How her lips pressed together in contained emotion.

"Don't do this," he pleaded, but she glanced away.

He stepped forward, needing to provide comfort, to touch her, to make sure he hadn't lost her already. Placing his shirt on the bed, he took the final step that separated them.

"This wasn't casual for me." He reached up to run his thumb over her cheek. The words weren't a declaration of love, and still, they were monumental for him. He hadn't put himself in a vulnerable position since Jessica, and going out on a limb was scary as shit.

Silence reigned as he willed Beth to really look at him. "I didn't think before I opened my mouth. I wanted to hurt my father, not you. I know that doesn't excuse what I said, but…"

He didn't know what else to say. He wasn't known for apologies. He rarely made mistakes, so he never needed to use them.

"I'm fine with the impulsive sex, or one-night stand, or whatever you want to call it, Dean. What I don't appreciate is being used to get back at your father."

He tilted his head, putting his face in her line of vision, and swallowed awkwardly at the glassy sheen in her eyes. "Beth…" Christ, this was hard. "This thing between us has nothing to do with my father. It's about me and you. I have issues with my old man that will never be resolved, but I would never use you."

He swore and tried to search for the words to convince her. "I don't want this to be casual. I've cared about you for a long time, and I know you know that. Please just give me a chance to make it up to you."

He needed to make her understand without scaring the shit out of her. He needed to prove it to her, but how?

"Spend the weekend with me," he blurted, the sudden epiphany seeming like an exceptional idea.

"No way." Her reply was immediate, adamant, and punctuated with a shake of her head.

He couldn't hold back the chuckle that burst free. He got a kick out of the ease in which she turned him down. "Spend the *day* with me," he counter-offered, this time boosting the effect with his trademark smile and dimples.

She continued to shake her head. "No. You need to go." She reached for his shirt and pushed it to his chest.

Ignoring her, he stepped closer, their toes touching, his clothes now squashed between them. "I want to stay. I want to spend more time with you."

She regarded him as if he were dim-witted. "No."

Determination sparked in her eyes as she gave him a push back. His feet didn't move and she huffed in frustration, but stayed in place. She was caving. If she didn't want him here, she would've walked away by now. But here she stood, looking at him with defiance, trying to stare him down as his smile grew.

Who would back down first?

He grabbed his shirt from her hand and let it fall to the floor, hoping to tempt her with an unrestricted display of skin. He didn't bother to take note of where the material fell, instead concentrating on the way she clamped her lips tighter, trying to hold back the smile he could see in her eyes.

She raised her brows and finally stepped back. "Well, have fun driving home half naked."

A stronger man would have let her leave, grabbed his shirt from the floor, and given her space. But she made him weak and needy in the hottest possible way. He'd had a taste of her, and now he burned for more. He needed to put his hands on her, to take advantage of her feistiness and sate his will to stroke her delicate skin.

He captured her by the waist, spinning her without effort. She let out a gasp, then a high-pitched squeal as he gracelessly threw her onto the bed.

Her body bounced from the impact, hair, legs, and arms flying in different directions. She righted herself, hastily moving on her knees to glare at him, while he regarded her with predatory intent.

They fought to stare each other down, her posture changing to a prepared stance, as if he would pounce on her at any moment. Then her focus strayed, moving down his bare chest to his groin and the member of his anatomy that wanted to wave to her with enthusiasm.

"Oh no." Her eyes shot back to his, a slight blush reddening her cheeks. She shook her head with determination. "I'm not sleeping with you again."

Really?

He wasn't convinced. Maybe not today or tomorrow, but one day soon he would make sure they made love again. "I didn't ask you to. I only asked you to spend the day with me."

"Well, your little friend is voicing his own demands." She pointed her index finger at the bulge in his pants.

He smiled at her words and the breathy way they left her lips. "*Little* friend?" The blush on her cheeks darkened. "I didn't hear you complaining about his size earlier?"

She puffed out her chest, pretending to be fed up, and backed off the bed. "If you think I'm going to help inflate that oversize ego of yours, you can think again." She shooed him away with a flick of her wrist, a faint smile tilting the corners of her lips.

As she walked past, he grabbed her hand, entwining his fingers with hers and squeezing ever so gently. If playful teasing wouldn't work, he would take another route.

He let the humor fall away from his expression, replacing it with a heartfelt seriousness he hoped she believed. "Please, Beth. Let me spend the day with you."

# CHAPTER 7

*D*ean's fingers encased her wrist. The delicate hold ceased her movements and stopped her heartbeat altogether. Although he liked to play tough the majority of the time, the torment in his eyes made her acknowledge that maybe he was hurting, too.

The words he'd used with his father earlier had left her feeling cheap and dirty. He had rarely sworn in front of her. So the abrupt change in persona had hit with the force of a physical blow. Nevertheless, she accepted his apology and tried to convince herself he hadn't meant to hurt her.

Her forgiveness didn't mean she should spend the day with him though.

She could already feel the rapid beat of her pulse under the press of his fingers. More time with him would be a mistake, a supersized, colossal mistake.

The whole day together would only ensure more damage to her heart when things ended. Still she found herself wanting to agree. Then before she knew it, she had opened her mouth. "No sex."

He jerked his head in surprise, or maybe he was insulted

by the stipulation. He would probably renege on his plans if bumping uglies wasn't involved. She began to think he was about to reject her terms when his face brightened with smug satisfaction.

"No sex," he echoed with too much seduction to even consider his credibility. He knew he had the upper hand where sex and persuasion were concerned. The ass practically had the monopoly on the market, which meant she needed to be firm on the no nookie front.

She sighed in defeat and raised her gaze up his delicious chest. Who was she kidding? She couldn't turn down more time with him. She already wanted to lick a trail from his cum gutters, all the way up to his dark ruby nipples.

If only she could trust him to be true to his word.

Glancing back up to his face, she scrutinized him. She wasn't sure Captain Copulation could agree to a no-sex rule without his manhood shriveling away.

"You promise?" As much as her core clenched in protest, she needed to sort out her feelings for him before they dived between the sheets again.

"No sex. Scout's honor." He held up his hand in what she assumed was a scout's pledge. She opened her mouth, prepared to surrender, but he cut her off. "Unless you beg for it."

She fixed him with a glare. "There will be no begging, Dean Sutherland."

Cocky bastard.

His self-confidence rubbed off on her and she felt empowered to do a little teasing of her own. His gaze followed her as she moved into him. With deliberate purpose she stared at his mouth provocatively, running her tongue over her lips in blatant invitation. A burst of pride warmed her belly when she noticed his Adam's apple bob.

Two could play this game.

"Unless you plan on begging," she whispered with a curve to her lips.

His head moved closer, continuing the seduction, taking the game to the next level. "I'm not too proud to beg." His mouth stopped millimeters from her ear, the warmth of his breath traveling down her neck, under her skin, and down her spine. "For you."

She could feel the movement of his lips against her hair as he whispered, the pleasure ripping a betraying moan from her throat before she could stop it.

Damn the man and his unwavering sex appeal.

She already wanted to cave and take back her stipulation. There was no way she could hold out for an extended period of time.

"So, does this mean you'll spend the day with me?"

She pretended to ponder the idea for a moment, glancing off into space while tapping her chin with her index finger.

He seemed happy to continue the charade by acting impatient. First his hands gripped her hips, then he walked his fingers up her sides, gently digging in to tease her ribs.

She hated being tickled, always had, but she loved his large hands on her body in equal measure. Even in torture his touch enslaved her.

Her body began to wiggle, her toes curling, unable to withstand the suffering. She gasped, trying to scream. "Y-yes. Yes, okay, I'll spend the day with you."

The pressure stopped immediately, his hands now lowering to rest on her hips. He gave a sincere smile, dimples showing and all, before doing the last thing she ever imagined a grown man would do. He fist pumped like a teenager. "*Yesss.*"

She threw her head back with a bark of laughter, the tension draining from her body. When she looked back at him, she could see legitimate happiness in his eyes.

She needed to believe it came from something deep and emotional, but her brain knew better. She had to keep reminding herself that things between them were only casual.

Before she could move away to hide her sudden melancholy, his lips were on hers, his tongue seeking immediate entrance in a devastating, passionate kiss that robbed her lungs of breath. She couldn't help reciprocating, kissing him back, clinging to his bare chest, savoring his tight hold as their tongues danced.

Her hands roamed, moving over his bare skin, to feel every curve, every hard plane. Talk about a lack of self-control. She'd never been the type to give in to temptation so easily; however, she found herself second-guessing every action around this man.

Clutching the bare thread of strength she had left, she smacked his chest. "I said no sex."

He frowned at her. "Babe, I hate to break it to you, but that was just a kiss."

She rolled her eyes and moved from his embrace to stalk toward her bathroom. "I'm taking a shower."

Alone time became increasingly necessary with each passing minute. Her body needed time to desensitize, to stop humming on an erotic level that continued to keep her blood on a slow boil.

"You're welcome to use the other bathroom down the hall if you plan on staying. And be aware, I have things to do today and I don't plan on changing my schedule."

"Yes, ma'am," he replied as she closed herself into the privacy of her bathroom and locked the door—just in case.

An hour later, she stood in Dean's home, peering through the floor-to-ceiling windows at the water of the Melbourne, Docklands below. His apartment stole her breath.

The heels of her sandals had clicked on the lavish black tiles of the entry hall while he held the thick wooden door open for her. Each tile flaunted unique wisps of silver that threaded through the gleaming surface, leading her into the open-plan dining, kitchen, and living area.

She had imagined him living in a bachelor pad, a shrine dedicated to his single status. But as she glanced around the tastefully decorated apartment, with its dark leather couches and large glass dining table, she realized she'd underestimated him.

He had expensive taste, art and furniture included. She never would have guessed he would be a neat freak as well. The kitchen's stainless-steel appliances gleamed. The charcoal marble bench tops were spotless and bare.

No, it definitely wasn't a bachelor's pad. This apartment spoke volumes about his maturity and pride and she felt another piece of her heart crumple under the weight of admiration.

On the drive here, she'd assured herself the large detour on the way to the grocery store wasn't anything to get worked up over. He needed to brush his teeth and change his clothes. He hadn't taken up the offer to shower at her house, stating he didn't want to intrude, and would freshen up at his place.

She didn't believe there were any ulterior motives to the quick visit, but seeing where he lived would have ramifications. His intimate hideaway would be another memory she would need to forget when things between them ended.

But she couldn't expect him to spend the day in his dirty

work clothes either. Okay, so maybe it would have been logical if he went by himself and met her back at her townhouse later. However, they only agreed to one day together. Merely a few hours to get to know each other on a friend to friend basis, and they couldn't do that properly if they spent the majority of the time apart.

While she convinced herself she was doing the right thing, she grasped a framed picture off the mantelpiece above the extravagant electric fireplace. The image was of Dean when he was a teenager, embracing a young girl, her beauty a feminine version of his own.

"My sister," he offered, coming up behind her.

"She looks sweet." She glanced over her shoulder to see him nodding, his gaze fixed on the image.

"Yeah, she is. Megan doesn't have a selfish or petty bone in her body. She's her mother's daughter, thank God, and nothing like our father."

She wanted to know the story behind his somber expression. She only feared he would close up on her if she prodded too hard.

"You two are close?"

His gaze met hers and she blindly placed the frame back on the mantel before turning to face him.

"Mmm." He nodded with a sad smile. "She didn't have the best father figure growing up, so I tried to make up for the loss. Megan looked up to me and I protected her from the real world as best I could. But she's a grown woman now, pregnant and happily married."

Dean a father figure? She smiled at the mental image. A young, strapping male growing up with the responsibilities of a man. No wonder he was so confident, so self-assured; he'd had to play the grown-up role from an early age.

"We were very close...are still very close. But that's

enough about me." His tone deepened as he leaned a little closer.

She tilted her head, bringing her lips closer to his. She didn't want his kiss and knew it would lead to something much sexier, yet she was unable to stop her actions.

"How about a guided tour?" He spoke into her mouth, teasing her with his proximity.

She should've said *no, hell no*, at the prospect of seeing his bedroom. Instead, she found herself nodding. She already had a library full of fantasies stored in her mind involving his private room. Her brain would need to do renovations, expanding shelf space, if she found out what it looked like in reality.

He grabbed her hand, bringing it to his lips for a soft kiss before entwining their fingers and leading her down the hall. Their connection hadn't been theatrical, just a simple peck, but the simplicity of his actions seemed monumental.

It felt like a moment between longtime lovers, not two people who shared one morning of passion. The intimate caress made her swallow down the butterflies multiplying like bunnies in her belly.

She was in so much trouble.

He leisurely led her through the apartment, giving her hand a soft squeeze every now and again. He explained the art on the walls, admitting his sister organized the majority of the furnishings, although he had the final say on all the purchases.

The first two bedrooms boasted floor to ceiling windows with captivating views of the Docklands. Each room had its own color theme, first a deep green with cream, the next navy and white. The furniture consisted of thick bed frames, dark polished dressers with expensive adornments, and matching bedside tables with stylish iron lamps.

He gave her a brief look into his study, the walls lined

with stocked bookshelves and a thick, wooden table in the center. When he shut the door behind them and led her to the one remaining room, she almost dragged her fingers from his grip.

He must have sensed her unease because he let her hand fall and gestured for her to walk in front. With timid steps she moved to the room where all the magic happened. She wondered if his personal room would be different from the others. Maybe with ladies' underwear hanging from the bedposts, or a corkboard filled with pictures of his conquests.

She knew the thoughts were ridiculous, yet a tiny piece of her hoped she was right.

It was unhealthy to continue seeing him as the perfect man. She needed something to dislike about him, something to focus on that didn't involve white picket fences, a family station wagon, and a very convenient happily ever after.

The intoxicating scent of his aftershave filled her lungs with each step. Chocolate brown adorned the wall behind the hardwood king-size bed, the shade a tone darker than his eyes. On the opposite wall stood a dressing table, tall and proud, with the space above holding a television bigger than the one in her living room.

"Wow, it's an honor to enter this infamous space." She tried to dislodge a twinge of jealousy over the women who had shared his bed.

"Let's hope you're the last."

She ground her teeth at the absurdity of his statement and glared over her shoulder. He must have a very low opinion of her if he thought she was that naive. He stood a few feet behind her, arms crossed casually over his chest, but his expression didn't hold the sarcasm she expected.

"Don't patronize me." She didn't know why his playful banter stung; it just did. "So how many ladies have made the cut?" The masochistic remark left her mouth before she thought better of it.

She didn't want to know. Her heart couldn't take the reality check.

"Too many." The rough reply hurt more than she anticipated. "You're the first woman I've ever had to beg to get here though." Her lips twitched at the memory. "I'm going to get ready. I won't be long."

He picked up a remote from his bedside table, turned on the television, then threw the remote onto the bed. "Make yourself at home."

She sat cautiously on the bottom edge of the mattress, her focus wavering, switching between the TV and Dean as he walked into his private bathroom.

He left the door wide open, giving her a perfect view of the open-ended shower, the sparkling tiles and gleaming taps. She assumed he would shower and change; only he made no effort to close the door, so she gathered he must be brushing his teeth.

It wasn't until he began to undress that she realized her assumption had been wrong.

His shirt came off in one fluid motion, the muscles of his back contorting and stretching as the material dropped to the floor. Before she comprehended what he was doing, his pants came down. Underwear, too.

She should have diverted her gaze, should have moved to the head of the bed, where his body would be out of view, but she couldn't. She focused on his body, the size of his thighs, the dip of his back just above his buttocks.

Oh God, did he think she couldn't see him?

Then with dawning brilliance she realized his plan.

The bastard was tempting her, trying to make her beg for sex. It had been working too; her body already hummed with desire, pleading to be sated one more time. Too bad Dean and her libido were going to be left unsatisfied. She wouldn't give in so easily. No matter how lickable his muscles were or how much she ached for his touch.

Not. Gonna. Happen.

If he wanted to put on a show, so be it. It wasn't like half the attractive women on this side of the hemisphere hadn't already seen him naked. She may as well take advantage of the free entertainment. Hell, maybe he was an exhibitionist. Good for him. Today would be his lucky day, because she would be more than happy to watch from a distance.

In fact, she felt confident enough to blatantly watch from a much closer viewpoint.

As he stepped under the shower's spray, she walked toward the bathroom and stopped inside. She stood in riveted fascination, following the trail of water down the smooth, sculpted planes of his chest and down his thighs.

He turned to face her, his perusal casual, not showing a hint of surprise as his hand left a trail of body wash over his chest. His hair had darkened under the water, the loose lengths now draped around his face, framing charcoal eyes.

Faking a bravado she didn't have, she walked to the basin and pushed herself onto the vanity for a more comfortable position.

The shower's steam misted the air, traveling over her skin, under her knee-high skirt, and across the tops of her breasts. The warmth seeped into her, matching the fire burning between her legs, and she wished like crazy she could rub her thighs together.

She would not give in. This wasn't her first fight with temptation where he was concerned, and she doubted it would be the last.

In a trance, she followed his movements as he worked a lather over his body. His hand glided from his pecs, rubbing the muscles of his stomach, and then going farther down to the nest of curls at his groin.

When he cupped his balls, she sucked in a breath, gripping the vanity tight until her fingers screamed in protest. She couldn't look into his eyes, embarrassment would burn her cheeks if she did. But she could feel his stare on her, watching, noticing how her body hummed and shivered all at the same time. She couldn't help it, couldn't hide it.

He took his time, rubbing his palm back and forth, back and forth over his length. "Enjoying the show?" His hand continued to torment the flesh she tried to divert her attention from.

"I didn't realize you were providing entertainment otherwise I would have brought snacks." The words came out etched in confidence even though each syllable scraped over her raw throat. She couldn't allow him to break her resolve.

He chuckled, the deep tone of his voice making her core clench, her nipples harden. "I'll take pleasure in entertaining you." And with that, he angled around for more body wash.

Unable to resist staring, she looked at him, really looked at him. Even semi-erect he was remarkably well hung. He didn't seem to be staying that way though. When he turned back around his cock had already grown, now jutting from his thighs like hard steel.

She itched to reach out and touch, to run her fingers over his flesh and see if the length moved in response. The scent of him became heavier, the aroma from the body wash filling her nose, her lungs, her soul. She'd loved that smell, imagined inhaling the tangy and commanding mix even when he wasn't around.

It was his scent. His essence.

He grabbed himself in one hand and began to stroke his length. From root to tip, his palm ran back and forth, back and forth while she stared in wanton fascination. His expression intensified, the lines and angles of his features more clear-cut and tense.

He focused on her like a predator. "You sure you don't want to join me?"

She cleared her throat then shook her head, unable to voice a response. Even if she could speak, she wouldn't trust her mouth to say the right thing. Her hormones were currently cat fighting with her restraint, trying to viciously shred it to pieces.

Without pausing his strokes, he turned toward her in the shower, resting his spare hand against the glass. His shoulders slumped, his stance widening as if he fought for strength or control.

"Come here," he growled, the sound so deep it barely registered over the noise of the rushing water.

She shook her head, adamant on maintaining her position on the bench. Right here was fine, out of touching distance, out of the zone of utter temptation. But her legs betrayed her as they began scissoring inches off the floor, aching to move toward him.

"Please, just come to the glass."

Her hesitation was lame at best. She scooted off the vanity and her feet slowly shuffled forward of their own volition.

Their gaze remained locked the entire time, each step making her weaker, taking her closer to the hypnotic intensity of his eyes.

She couldn't resist the scorching need of this man. He had the confidence to beg, didn't shy away from his lust, and being the woman to cause such strong emotions was all consuming. It made her wonder if he always acted this way. Did every woman he slept with experience this hunger? This raw need?

She moved to the glass in front of him, a mere step away

from the shower's opening. They were so close, but she wanted to be closer. She wanted to be on the other side of the glass, his heated touch scorching a trail over her naked flesh.

Raising a shaky hand, she placed it on top of his through the barrier separating them. Unable to see the way he worked himself due to their proximity, she drowned in his eyes, aware that his hand had increased in pace by the movement of his upper arm.

Her heart pounded. Her throat was dry and rough as sandpaper as her core clenched, demanding attention. She needed to leave, to end the battle of wills and stop making things between them more complicated. How could any other man compare or live up to the sensations she now associated with passion and lust?

"Talk to me." He tilted his head forward to rest against the glass.

"I-I..." She shook her head. She was acting like a nun, unable to speak or think or breathe. "I don't know what to say." She bit the inside of her mouth in frustration. She wanted to please him, but her inhibitions held her back. She licked her lips, and he responded with a groan, loud and long.

"Your mouth drives me crazy." He dropped his head back, eyes closing for a second before his gaze returned to hers.

She copied his stance, moving so her forehead rested against his. Millimeters separated them, yet they were so far apart, and still, his raw expression empowered her to say the words she'd been withholding.

"Come for me," she breathed. Heat saturated her cheeks.

His chest rumbled, primitive and fierce. His upper arm now moved in frantic motions while his eyes called for her to join him. She wouldn't. She couldn't risk falling for him any more than she already had. Even if it meant her body remained raw and sensitive. Keeping her job was more important than casual sex with a man who would never love her.

"Say it again," he commanded.

"Come for me." Her voice became louder, more forceful as they stared at each other, sharing the most erotic moment of her life.

Without warning he threw his head back, his hair mingling with the water's spray, her name leaving his lips on a moan.

She glanced down at the hand frantically working his cock. She stared, inquisitive and aroused beyond her wildest dreams while his seed landed on the glass separating them. He continued to work himself, his strokes short and sharp at the head of his shaft.

Her gaze didn't leave his sex as his movements slowed. Damn, she needed a relief, just a little respite from the hyper-awareness of her body. Even her nipples ached from the friction of her bra.

"Jesus Christ." His palm stopped stroking.

She stepped back, breaking the hypnosis, retreating from the intensity to gain her composure. However, she couldn't tear her gaze from him.

She breathed deeply, slowing the rapid pace of her heart while he positioned his body under the shower spray, washing himself off and splashing water on the glass before wrenching the taps off.

In a flash of movement, he maneuvered his chest around the glass, grabbed her arm, and pulled her into the shower stall.

She squealed in protest. The abrupt capture made her feel like a mouse in the lion's den. Her heart took off at a gallop, and she had a moment to catch her breath before he placed her against the wet, tiled wall.

Instead of pushing away, trying to distance herself, she clung to him. Her hands gripped his hard triceps, her lips tilted up to meet his as he moved in to devour her mouth. Teeth clashed, tongues collided, his dominating, hers submitting as they writhed together.

Water from his body and the glass seeped into her clothes, cooling her skin, yet it didn't douse the fire in her belly. The contrast only made her hotter.

Without warning he leaned back, breaking the connection. He stared into her eyes, his face contorted with a frown. "I can't believe you didn't beg."

She laughed.

He boasted heated passion one minute and cheeky flirt the next. If only he knew how close she'd been to conceding defeat.

Stroking a lock of soaked hair from his forehead, she smiled at him. "Maybe you've lost your Midas touch."

He inched forward, his gaze sharp, scrutinizing her. If he kissed her again she would cave. She would hitch her skirt up and beg to be taken. But his face diverted at the last moment to nuzzle his nose into her neck, hitting the sensitive spot at the join of her shoulder.

"Maybe I just need to try a little harder," he whispered.

His breathy declaration tightened around her heart and her responding chuckle came out awkward. "Or maybe we should leave."

<h1 style="text-align:center">CHAPTER 8</h1>

*B*eth in her business suit and high heels turned him on like nobody's business. Seeing her in casual clothes, her body on display in skintight material, caused his cock to ache relentlessly.

The black ruffled skirt currently hugging her fine ass finished just above her knees. It was the entire reason he'd been walking behind her as they strolled up and down the grocery aisles. Not that he didn't enjoy the view from the front. The baby pink sports singlet fit her like a glove, showing off an impressive figure, her trim belly and small, firm rack.

She looked completely transformed from the woman he salivated over in the office. She even held herself differently, her smile more like a devilish grin, her eyes conspiring and more mischievous than the professional businesswoman from Sutherland & Son.

He couldn't decide which side he loved more, the confident, sophisticated femme fatale or the playful, tempting bombshell. And holy fuck, he had used the L-word without conscious thought. Nothing shriveled up a man's package more than the L-word or the commitment that usually came with it. Yet he still felt as hot as a firecracker.

He tried to shake it off, occupying himself with the unanswered question that had plagued him for the last few hours. Was she wearing a G-string or going without panties altogether?

If he considered her modesty, the way she blushed in heated situations and the usual G-string panty line under her suits, he would guess G-string. But the damn woman was hot as Hades today.

Her heated whisper of *Come for me* still echoed in his ears and the thought of her wearing no panties made him want to try all the harder to find out.

He still couldn't believe she'd watched him in the shower. He intentionally left the door open, thinking his nudity would embarrass her. He hadn't anticipated her enjoying the performance.

And he never knew grocery shopping could be this enjoyable. He'd spent the last ten minutes constantly staring at the firmest, most mouth-watering ass he'd ever had the pleasure of admiring.

His housekeeper usually stocked his cupboards and fridge. He only needed to get the occasional milk or bread. This experience, however, was something he wanted to do more often.

She stopped a few feet ahead, causing him to snap back to reality. With reluctance he removed his gaze from her delectable curves to take a cursory glance at what she would put in the basket next. Only she hadn't paused to put anything in. She peered over her shoulder, catching his stare as it left her butt.

He waited for the indignant expression, not having to

pause long before he received it. He smiled back, attempting to seem innocent. Apparently, he wasn't all that convincing, because she raised her brows and rolled her eyes.

The slight tilt to her lips as she turned away didn't escape him though, and she continued down the aisle with an added swing to her step. She loved the attention as much as he loved giving it.

He didn't know why she fought their attraction. Okay, maybe he did. His reputation was an obstacle they needed to overcome. Since Jessica he hadn't bothered paying attention to women, unless they were in his bedroom, or in an effort to get them there. His father had made him bitter—resentful— and his hatred for the opposite sex had taken a while to simmer down.

Beth had changed him. Her unwavering kindness and exuberance made him feel like Mary Poppins or some shit, seeing a ray of sunshine at the end of the freaking tunnel.

As he followed her past the cold section, he grabbed a can of whipped cream, feeling the need to push the boundaries one more time. When he caught up to her he held up the can and raised his brows.

He would have wagered good money on her blushing and telling him to put it back, perhaps even taking the time to remind him of the no-sex rule. She surprised him again. Instead of arguing, she merely shook her head in resignation and watched him place the can with the rest of the groceries.

This could be the green light he'd been looking for. Maybe he should take a turn back down the chocolate fudge aisle and get all the ingredients to make a proper meal out of her.

Two aisles later, he had his mind stuck in a strange mental space. His thoughts drifted from the human chocolate sundae to things of a more permanent nature.

Could he do this every weekend? Grocery shopping with

her like a normal couple? He had no doubt they would be great together. He enjoyed her company, she was passionate in bed, and her beauty—

"Dean?"

He glanced up to see her frowning at him. "Sorry?"

"Are you staying for dinner? I'll buy something for us to eat if you are."

Well, maybe his Midas touch wasn't broken after all. At least he didn't have to beg for an invitation.

"Love to." For the life of him he couldn't stop staring at her as if she would be on the menu. "Don't worry about cooking, though. I'll buy takeout. How does Chinese sound?"

"Dean? Dean Sutherland?" The feminine voice came from behind him, sending an unwelcome shiver down his spine. His mind couldn't put a face to the tone, but without looking he knew he wouldn't want to introduce the woman to Beth.

With hesitation he accepted the inevitable and turned to find not one, but two ladies sauntering forward from the end of the aisle.

Not good.

Not good at all.

Their bright smiles and postage stamp tops greeted him, making him freak the fuck out.

Seriously? *Seriously.*

When would he catch a break?

And how the hell did he introduce them to Beth—*Hey, sweetheart, I'd like you to meet the ladies who popped my threesome cherry. This is Britney and shit, sorry, what was your name?*

This would *not* go down well.

"Ladies," he greeted with a nod, trying to be civil while wanting to run like fuck. He couldn't remember the other woman's name. Not that he had plans of making introductions. He hoped the quick greeting would be sufficient before he could flee.

Britney's smile widened and she practically skipped toward him, big boobs bouncing as if trying to break free from her tiny top. Without a glance in Beth's direction she ambled forward, planting a kiss on his cheek that lasted longer than the fucking bicentennial. Her roommate had the decency to stand back, content to give him seductive looks from a few feet away.

What the hell could he say to them when they only had a threesome in common?

*So, how's that flexibility of yours going?*

"What are you lovely ladies up to?" He hoped Beth would consider him more of a well-mannered gentleman for not giving them the brush-off.

"I was just telling Stacy how boring tonight was going to be because we don't have any plans." A pout spread Britney's tacky glossed lips while she tried to work him with her innocent eyes. She couldn't fool the blind. The woman didn't have an ounce of innocence left. "Maybe you could come over and the three of us could have another private party."

Warning bells sounded, loud and clear in his skull as she stroked a finger down his chest. He glanced at Beth, wanting to explain but she had already turned and started walking away.

*Great.*

Just when his fantasies of whipped cream and fudge sauce were about to become a reality.

He huffed and glared down at Britney. The woman was a leech, and she knew damn well that he already had company.

"Sorry, not interested," he growled, biting back the need to yell in frustration.

Her lusty expression turned to shock as he grabbed her wrist and dropped it away from his chest. No doubt this was the first time she'd been rejected because she seemed to have problems understanding the concept.

"Look, I've gotta go." He gave a two-finger wave to Britney's friend, whose name he'd already forgotten, and started walking.

Talk about your private parts shriveling. His nuts were practically burrowing their way into his gut, searching for sanctuary in case Britney caused a scene. He heard her sputter and scoff, but didn't bother to look back as he went in search of Beth.

After five minutes of walking the aisles he found her at the checkouts, placing items on the conveyor with more determination than necessary. She was upset and didn't bother to make eye contact when he moved to stand beside her.

"Sorry about that." He had nothing else to offer. What did you say to the woman you were trying to impress after running into your old threesome buddies?

"No problem." She focused her attention on unloading the groceries.

He grabbed the remaining items, the whipped cream included, and placed them on the conveyor. He noticed how she watched the can, staring in a daze for a moment before she frowned and looked away.

Back to square one again by the looks of it.

He grabbed her hand, entwining their fingers as he'd enjoyed doing earlier. Her gaze darted from their joined fingers, to his eyes, before she turned her back to him.

Leaning in, he inhaled the sweet smell of her perfume and let his voice whisper over her neck. "You okay?"

Her exhale was audible, the emotional exhaustion hitting his ears to give him a heavy dose of guilt. "Perfect."

*Bullshit.*

They both knew she was lying. He had no plans of letting it fly. The idea of spending the rest of the afternoon in awkward silence or uncomfortable conversation didn't sit well with him.

"You're upset."

She had already put on her indifferent mask, hiding behind a tight smile and placating eyes.

"No. I'm just being silly." She turned to face the checkout attendant, clearly wanting to drop the subject.

Did he take the hint? Hell no; he lapped up her displeasure. He squeezed her hand, giving a little tug until she turned back to face him with a huff.

"You're jealous." He couldn't contain himself; he grinned like a lunatic. She may have been coping with her feelings in the sweetest way possible, trying to change the subject and move on, but she *was* jealous.

Her eyebrows pulled together, and she stared into the distance over his shoulder. "They're beautiful."

The awe in her voice hit him like a kick in the balls. She spoke as if her own beauty was inferior.

He leaned in close and placed a peck on her cheek. He ached to kiss her lips, to pull their bodies together and reassure her with actions instead of words, but he didn't want to weaken the conversation by turning it into a heated make-out session.

"Yeah, they're attractive…in a cheap and easy kind of way. You, Beth, are beautiful." He marked his words by moving over to kiss her other cheek. "Naturally gorgeous." Another kiss to her jaw. "Remarkably alluring." He added a final nip to the low of her neck.

He moved his head back and stared into her eyes, trying to convey his sincerity. Christ, she was exquisite, the most mesmerizing woman he'd ever seen, and she had no clue.

She shook her head with a dramatic roll of her eyes. "You're smooth. Real smooth."

He fixed her with a smirk, happy with himself for making

her smile. He wanted to lean in and kiss her again, on the lips this time. Before he had the chance, the moment was broken by the checkout attendant.

"That'll be seventy-eight dollars and twenty cents, thanks."

CHAPTER 9

*H*ours later Beth sat on her upstairs balcony, a glass of wine in hand and a sense of cluelessness clouding her brain. The sun's rays dwindled, the warmth of the day becoming chilly as night crept into the sky.

She had spent the afternoon trying not to let the tall, slim, and stacked women from the supermarket ruin her day. It was a rare occurrence to sleep with the man of your dreams, or have the pleasure of watching him grease the sprocket in the shower. She'd gone too far to let reality seep in now.

If only she could forget the comment about the three of them having a *private party*.

The bile that had risen up her throat at the syrupy way the leggy blonde cooed at him still soured her mouth. The thought of him sharing himself with one woman at a time had been painful enough. She'd never contemplated him having multiple partners at once. Her ignorance proved just how far out of her depth she was.

Although she thought her knowledge of him was fairly thorough, the last twenty-four hours had been a revelation. She had learned so much about him, yet she had no idea how he felt toward her or if his intentions were only focused on sex.

She loved the way his teasing brought a smile to her face she couldn't seem to wipe off. Buying the whipped cream, for instance.

While she busied herself with unpacking the groceries, he had scavenged through each bag. The next thing she knew, the burst of sound from the pressure-filled can had echoed off the kitchen walls. When she turned in surprise, he was right behind her, his index finger covered in cream, which he then ran along her lips.

She didn't have a chance to move back or lick the sweetness away before his mouth was over hers, doing the task for her.

They had stumbled over half-empty grocery bags as he backed her into the corner of the kitchen. Then without effort he lifted her to sit atop the counter and began devouring her mouth, his force and demanding desire making her sex throb.

"What are you thinking?" his voice snapped her back to the present.

She watched in a lazy stare while he took a swig of his beer, waiting for a reply. The glow from the tea light candles made his dark eyes appear deep and menacing. Wisps of hair were loose around his forehead, and he sat back in his chair looking comfortable and content, not only in his own skin, but in her home.

Her cheeks heated, the gradual flame burning hotter while she remembered what she'd been thinking about, the way his tongue and lips had removed every last bit of cream.

"Nothing," she lied, trying not to smile.

"Still sticking to your no-sex rule?" He took another lazy drink from the bottle.

Her cheeks flamed red-hot at his direct question. It didn't

help that she was blazing up from the inside out, the heat most potent between her thighs.

"Dean." She raised her brows in warning.

His sultry lips mocked her as they glistened from the beer, begging to be licked. If only she could throw caution to the wind and enjoy what was right in front of her.

His face turned contemplative as he took another swig from the bottle, his eyes downcast when he spoke. "We'd be good together, Beth."

She sighed, unable to let the unease rest in her chest. They *would* be good together, for a time at least. But what would happen when he grew tired of having sex with the same woman? Because there was no way in hell she would sleep with him even on a casual basis without them being exclusive.

Were they both adult and emotionally stable enough to return to an amicable relationship when things ended? She didn't think so. She would be forced to leave her job, not necessarily by Dean, but by the heartache of seeing him every day.

She paused, biting into a piece of cheese and taking a sip of wine, before answering. She wanted to believe his interest was more than sexual, more than casual, if only he had given her the words to confirm it. He was either sincere, laying his heart on the line, or doing a damn fine job playing her.

As she chewed and swallowed, her heart fought to convince her mind, and her mind continued to second-guess. In the end she decided to play off the seriousness of his state-ment with a jovial reply.

"Yes, we would be a truly great couple." She gave a humorless chuckle. "You with your inability to commit and me with my inability to trust."

They fell silent, the sound of crickets and cars driving in the distance the only noise. His beauty was undeniable.

Never had a man been so perfect in her eyes. And she wanted to believe him, wanted to believe *in* him; she just didn't have the confidence to let go of all her doubts.

A man proud of playing the field didn't change overnight, yet she needed to believe he was capable of turning over a new leaf. She wanted his feelings for her to be strong enough to break his habit of one-night stands. That he could desire her enough to change the person he was into the person she needed him to be.

Unfortunately, her life didn't resemble a fairy tale and he wouldn't be turning into her prince or knight in shining armor or whatever else her fantasies needed him to be.

"I've wanted you for a long time—"

"And you had me." She didn't need to hear the speech again. The words hadn't skipped her attention the first time.

She slipped from her seat to put distance between them. She walked to the railing of the balcony and rested her back against the wood. The extra space made speaking with him easier, to be able to look at him without his gaze feeling like a caress. "I enjoyed this morning just as much as you did. It scratched an itch we both had. But I'm not into casual sex."

His frown deepened as he took another stern chug of his beer. His shoulders straightened and his nostrils flared while his dominant, masculine vibes surrounded her.

"Well, my itch is far from being scratched." He placed the bottle on the table with a thud and moved to his feet.

Her lungs constricted at his approach and he didn't stop until they were a foot apart. His stare seeped under her skin as he leaned in, a lock of hair falling down to cover one eye, and he placed his hands on the railing on either side of her. "I want you. Not just for the night, or the morning, or whatever else you think. I want *you*...I want *me* and *you*."

He leaned closer, his lips brushing hers, the mix of beer

and heat and man mingling on her tongue, sizzling her veins. "No other woman has made me want to beg."

Another kiss brushed her mouth while his hips settled against hers. "No other woman, Beth."

Her lips parted on a moan, eagerly anticipating his kiss, and all the fight drained from her body. There was no more strength of will, no more self-preservation.

She could feel his erection through the material of his jeans, and couldn't find a reason to deny herself any longer. She wanted him. Wanted to spend the night making love to him, having sex with him, whatever he wanted to classify it as, just as long as his body was between her thighs, dulling the ache.

"Let's order food."

She paused in confusion and mentally shook herself. Food? Her body hummed, her panties were damp, and he was talking about food. Hadn't he just been kissing her, grinding himself into the softness of her belly?

"I promised you no sex, remember?"

She growled. Yeah, she remembered. It flashed like a neon sign in her mind.

$\mathcal{D}$ean had never shared a meal with another person and enjoyed the experience as much as he just had with Beth.

Over dinner, their usual comfortable mockery had been emphasized with the buzz of a few beers and a bottle of wine, and he couldn't help but find her happiness contagious. His focus was glued to her, firmly stuck on the smile plastered on her face while he helped clear away the dirty plates.

The banter during the meal had left them both clutching their ribs in laughter and his cheeks were already sore from smiling. He loved making her laugh. There wasn't a sweeter sound. The noise filled him with a strange sense of pride that a man like himself could make a woman like her happy in any sort of way.

Once the main meal was finished she had risen from her seat and walked toward him with the box of fortune cookies. He'd sat in silence, resting back in his chair, noticing how her cheeks turned a soft shade of pink with her approach.

She moved in beside him, clearing space on the table to take a seat in front of him. Her gorgeous legs crossed provocatively, causing her skirt to hitch up her thighs. His mouth dried, and he struggled to clear his throat. He didn't speak, didn't want to scare her off as she broke apart small pieces of fortune cookie and shyly bent at the waist to place them in his mouth.

They fed one another, the previous playful moment now replaced with a growing intensity that turned him hard as stone.

Christ, he wanted her. He was dying to get between her legs, to run his fingers over her soft flesh and taste her essence. To make her thrash with need and scream his name. He only had to push up her skirt, turn her legs toward him, and let his wandering hands do the rest.

The mere thought made him itch to palm his cock. His sex drive had always been strong, even on his weakest days, but never like this. He needed her with a hunger so fierce it ate him from the inside out.

What surprised him the most was the new appetite he hadn't experienced before. He wanted to simply hold her, to drown in the sweet scent of her hair and run gentle fingers along her creamy white skin.

The craving to simply be with her equally matched his sexual appetite. He wanted to drown in the sea-green depths of her eyes and feel the heat spread through his veins when she smiled, her eyes crinkling, her tiny dimples showing.

"Are you ready to watch a movie?"

Her voice startled him. He'd been staring at the tablecloth like a dickhead, lost in his own little world.

"Yeah, sounds good."

She led the way into the living room and bent over to grab the remote from the coffee table. "What type of movie do you want to watch?"

He honestly didn't care. If he had her snuggled in his arms he would even agree to a chick flick. "You deci—" His cell phone vibrated in his pants pocket and he pulled it out to check the caller ID—Megan—his sister.

"Do you mind if I take this?" He made a conscious effort to ignore work calls today, but preferred not to ignore his sister. When your father was a bastard, you tended to hold tight to the remaining family you had left.

"Go ahead. I'll make some popcorn."

She made her way from the room while he sank onto the couch and answered the call. His sister hadn't uttered a word before his heart began pounding in his throat, her uncontrollable sobs shaking his foundation.

"Megan, what's wrong?"

In the seconds before she replied his thoughts went into a tailspin. Had something happened to his mother? His father? Then he remembered her pregnancy and his palms started to sweat.

"It…it's Tina…" Her voice broke in anguish.

Tina?

He frowned while his brain jumped to a thousand different conclusions. He had no clue who she was talking about. He could only remember one Tina, Megan's best friend from high school, but he hadn't heard anything about her in years.

"She's dead." The words came out in a choked cry and his heart skipped a beat.

He clutched the phone to his ear and closed his eyes, wishing he stood beside her instead of them being hours apart. He pushed from the couch and paced the room, his body demanding action, commanding he do something, anything.

"What happened, Meg? Where are you?"

"H-her car…s-she fell asleep…" Another sob had his fingers encircling the phone tighter, fighting the urge to crush the plastic into tiny little pieces.

"Where are you?" he demanded, wanting to get to her, to hold and protect her.

Her cries continued, her agony piercing him like a knife. He treasured his sister and couldn't stand the ache building in his chest knowing she was hurting.

When Megan's sobs grew faint, echoing into the background, a man's voice came over the line. "Dean?"

"Mark? What the hell is going on?" He glanced up, noticing Beth cautiously enter the room, her brow wrinkled with concern while Megan's husband spoke.

"It's okay," Mark assured. "We found out Tina passed away a few hours ago. I'm trying to keep Megan calm for the baby's sake, but nothing I do is working. I thought talking to you might help, but she's inconsolable. I don't know what else to do."

*Fuck.* He planted his feet and tried to calm his mind so he could think. Where were his keys? "I'm on my way."

"No. Don't. She'll be all right. You wouldn't be able to get here before morning anyway, and Megan will hate herself for making you come all this way. Once she gets some rest and isn't dealing with the shock, I know she'll settle down."

He was thankful his sister had found someone like Mark to look after her. Dean had spent many of his younger years taking care of her, being the father she needed, and he now found it hard to let go. He hadn't been the person she turned to for guidance or support for a long time, but Megan would always be his baby sister, and he didn't think he would ever stop picturing her as a fragile little girl.

"Can you put her back on?" He swallowed over the dryness in his mouth.

"Yeah sure, hold on a sec."

He waited, paused in Beth's hallway as he roughly ran a hand through his hair, pulling at the lengths in frustration. What the hell should he do? When Megan picked up the phone, his relief was palpable. She had stopped sobbing, her grief now expressed through soft sniffles and ragged exhales.

"Megan? I know you're hurting, and I wish more than anything in the world that I could be there with you, but you need to listen, okay? You need to be strong."

A strangled cry echoed through the phone into his chest. The noise penetrated his soul, making his eyes burn.

Not willing to share his weakness with Beth, he walked farther down the hall, opened the front door, and sat on the steps of her porch. "Listen, you have a beautiful baby to care for. And I know it's hard, but you need to stay strong for the little one." He paused, thankful to receive a sniff and mewled affirmation in reply.

"Now when you hang up the phone, tell Mark to run you a warm bath. Grab one of those romantic Sheikh books you love and try to relax. I know you're surrounded with horrible thoughts at the moment, but you need to drown in the good memories. Think about the happy times, the ones that made you laugh."

He prodded his forehead with strong fingers, trying to rack his brain for a memory of his little sister and her best friend. Vivid images of them scheming and laughing filled his mind, but he couldn't grasp a specific memory.

"Okay." Her voice was weak.

"How about the crush Tina used to have on David Wilkins?" He was clutching at straws, but the memory was better than nothing. "Remember the time he came over to study with me for a math exam and the two of you stalked him the whole time? The guy refused to come back to our house after that. Tina ended up leaving a love letter in his locker, didn't she?"

He received a half-sobbed chuckle in reply. "Yeah, she made me put it in there. She was too scared to get caught."

"Try and remember all those fun times for me. Try and

think of the best memories you have. Then write them down. And I know you need to cry, hon; I know you're hurting; just make sure you breathe. Make sure you stay strong for that little niece of mine."

Megan sniffed. "Or nephew."

"Yeah, or nephew. Although I'm convinced it's a girl."

He rested his head in his palm while silence stretched between them. He wished he knew what to say to ease her grief, to take the pain away and make her smile, even just for a little while.

"Thanks," she whispered.

"I love you, Sis."

"I love you, too," she replied. "I'm going to go. Mark's already running me a bath. I just needed to hear your voice."

"Be strong, Meg."

The call disconnected leaving him in deafening silence, weighed down by the heaviness in his chest. Megan was twelve when their father cheated on their mother, tearing apart the family and leaving Dean to be the man of the house. He hadn't been the best role model, hadn't always known what to do or say, but at least he stuck around.

Behind him the door creaked, announcing Beth as she approached. He took a moment to gain his composure, rubbing the back of his hand over his eyes while he breathed deep and stood.

"Sorry." She cringed. "I didn't mean to intrude. I just wanted to check to see if you were all right."

He moved toward her, needing her strength. Picking up her hand, he stared at the delicate skin and could only see the image of his crying sister. He didn't think he could stay away and rely on Mark to take care of her.

As he raised Beth's knuckles to his lips, he tried to convince himself Megan's husband would be enough. The guy had to be enough.

"Do you want to talk about it?" Her voice was filled with compassion, penetrating his wayward thoughts.

He gently pulled her into his chest, wrapped his arms around her waist, and let the delicate warmth of her body suffuse him. Holding her tight, he told her about his sister, about the loss of Tina and how she needed to stay strong for the baby.

She clung to him while he spoke in hushed whispers on her front porch. Not once did she waver in her hold or shift from foot to foot as if bored by his story. He didn't realize the way his shirt clung to him in patches until his words had dried up, her tears dampening the material.

Clutching her tighter, his heart grew heavy with gratitude. He would never be able to let her go. He wanted to keep her in his arms and could no longer imagine being without her.

He would always want her near, for comfort, for pleasure. For everything.

# CHAPTER 11

*B*eth hugged Dean's waist, her head resting on the firm planes of his chest. The frantic pulse of his heartbeat thrummed into her ear while her tears continued to fall.

His vulnerable side touched her in places she never thought feelings for Dean would reach. He had always been a fantasy and she held her barely contained lust for him very close. Now the dynamics had changed. He was real. A real man, with real feelings, not just a fantasy.

"Let's go inside." He placed a kiss on her forehead and loosened his grip.

As she moved out of his embrace, his fingers trailed down her arm, stopping at her hand, where he grasped it firmly, leading the way into the house. She didn't know what to do. Did he need space? She knew guys didn't do the whole emotional talking about feelings kind of thing, but ignoring what happened seemed wrong.

When he suggested starting a movie again, she agreed and chose a romantic comedy from one of the streaming sites. When the movie started, she walked back to the kitchen, fetching the now cold popcorn, another beer for Dean, and the remainder of her glass of wine.

"Sorry, the popcorn is cold. I'd make more but this was my last bag." She handed him the beer and tried to determine where to sit. The remainder of the night needed to be friendly, not flirty, so one of the single recliners would be best.

When she walked between him and the coffee table to reach her seat, he put his leg up, halting her passage. He gave her a somber smile and patted the spot beside him on the couch. "Come here."

She paused. She wasn't confident she could hide her need to touch him if she sat so close. With measured steps she took the position at his side, leaving room between them.

As she sank into the couch, just out of his reach, he leaned over, slid an arm around her waist, and pulled her closer until their bodies touched from knee to waist.

"I'm not hungry anyway," he whispered into her hair, "so you can have all the popcorn."

She clutched the bowl tighter, sinking into his body in small increments, trying to relax.

"I won't bite."

The graveled tone whispered over her neck, the sweep of his breath so close she could sense the slightest friction from his lips on her earlobe. She sank closer against him, not sure how to respond.

Guilt clawed at her. He grieved for his sister's friend, and yet she still couldn't dampen her lust. Her body already hummed, finely tuned to his proximity and every move he made. The reaction was all kinds of wrong, and she wished she could shut it off.

With waning concentration, she tried to focus on the movie, but scenes played without her notice. His hard thigh rested strong as steel beside her leg, his muscled arm around her shoulders, his scent mocking her restraint. She closed her eyes and struggled to shut out his presence.

When the male lead character made an arrogant comment about his remarkable good looks and prowess in bed, she couldn't help laughing. Dean had a doppelgänger.

"What's so funny, chuckles?" He tickled her neck, shocking a cry of laughter from her lips.

She squealed and turned toward him, moving her neck away from his torturing fingers. "Nothing."

He watched her through pained eyes and the sight stole her happiness, replacing it with a hollow ache in her belly. He continued to stare at her, his gaze penetrating and deep, while his hands moved down her shoulders, over her sides, along her hips. She bit her lip, unable to look away as his touch fell farther, moving to cup her bottom. He guided her movements, gripping her body until she straddled his lap.

She settled into him, face-to-face, the heat of her core against the hard length in his pants, and she fought to stop herself from leaning in to kiss him. He needed her, and whatever he wanted she would give. Her own desires were selfish at a time like this, so she waited, hoping he would set the pace.

There was nothing playful in his eyes. His lower lashes rested against hard shadowed skin and his lips were in a flat, lifeless line. He gripped her hips while they gazed at each other in silence.

No words were shared, but their connection spoke volumes. She could feel his grief, the churning anguish that stripped away his cocky persona and left her with someone raw and true.

His emotions sucked her in, calling her closer, deeper, until she felt her soul reaching out. With a delicate hand she stroked the loose strands of dark chocolate hair from his face. The short, silken lengths glided through her fingers while his gaze grew into something other than pain.

Her stomach muscles tensed; she tried to control her nervousness as she continued to trace the planes of his face. Once more she raked her fingers through his hair, then along his jaw, down his throat, over his collarbone.

Her mouth began to water with each teasing stroke, and all the while he sat motionless, his stare encouraging her to continue, his quiet intensity demanding more.

Was she reading his signals properly? Was he searching for intimacy?

Unsure whether she was doing the right thing, she trailed her fingers back to his face. She swallowed hard and skimmed her thumb over the heat of his lush bottom lip, gliding back across the top before moving along the seam.

The nip of his teeth sent the breath from her lungs, the lick of his tongue shooting sensations along her arms, down her belly, between her thighs. And still he didn't move. He kept his hands on her hips, the burn of his stare marking her periphery.

Dying for a taste of him, she leaned in, her heart thundering as his eyes closed, anticipating her kiss. Rather than do what he expected, she paused millimeters from his mouth and extended her tongue, licking the join of his lips and savoring the salty taste.

His eyes shot open, his sharp intake of breath exciting her before he pulled their bodies together with a strong arm around her waist. His mouth clashed with hers, his lips strong and determined as his tongue sought entrance.

One of his hands moved up her back while their lips moved together in a heated rush. His hold came around the back of her head, keeping her in place, denying her the ability to break the kiss, not that she would ever want to, while his other hand sneaked under her top to sear the skin at her lower back.

She absorbed his heat, feeding off it, craving more, until her mind could concentrate on nothing but the feel of his tongue in her mouth, his fingers on her back.

Grasping his head firmly with both hands, she pulled at his hair, each short, sharp tug responded to with a grinding of his hips against her core. Neither said a word when he broke the connection, roughly removing their shirts, before planting his lips back on hers.

She placed her hands on his chest, embedding her fingernails, pressing deeper. His large hands moved to her calves, over her thighs, and under her skirt. When his fingers grazed against her G-string, he stopped, not going any further.

Pulling back, she looked at him. His eyes were alive with a raging fire, the heat emanating from him making her burn. She knew why he stopped. She could see the question in his expression. He was waiting for her to rescind the no sex rule.

Placing her lips back over his, she rose from his lap. "Take them off."

Without further instruction he tugged the material down over her bottom until they sat at midthigh. He left her G-string in the half-removed position and ran a hand up her rib cage to cup a breast through the material of her bra. With the other hand he continued to explore under her skirt.

His fingers glided to the apex of her thighs, then with a featherlight touch he stroked her intimate flesh, making her whimper without thought. The sensation rippled through her body, becoming more potent. His fingers parted her sex, moving deeper to stroke up and down, up and down, making her hips undulate and demand penetration.

Both of his hands left her body, then came back to rest on her ass, holding her tight, ensuring she didn't fall as he guided her to stand on shaky legs. She watched him scoot forward to the edge of the couch, undo his jeans and raise himself to lower them over his ass. Once they were at mid-thigh, he stood beside her then shucked his jeans and underwear completely until he was naked before her.

Leaning toward her coffee table, he picked up the remote and shut off the television with a soft click. He studied her face, the muscles of his jaw tight as his fingers played with her bra straps. "You sure you want this?"

Time to contemplate had long passed. She *did* want this.

With a nod, she stepped into him, her arms circling his waist, her nails running up his spine. His hands went around her back and with a flick of his fingers her bra came undone. He guided the straps down her arms, his appreciative gaze and reverent touch filling her with pride.

She still couldn't understand how he could make her feel so beautiful without a single word.

When her bra fell to the floor he picked her up in a gush of movement, one arm under her knees while the other held her back, to lay her down on the couch.

"Shit," he swore under his breath and backed away.

He turned to search the floor before he picked up his jeans and dug into one of his pockets. When he returned he placed a condom packet on her belly and positioned himself between her legs.

She shuddered over the possibilities. The inevitabilities. She needed this more than air.

He ran both hands up her legs, under her skirt, reaching the underwear halfway down her thighs. His fingers hooked underneath the elastic before he pulled them down, all the way off, then went back to do the same with her skirt.

His gaze ate up her naked body, pausing at the trimmed curls at her mound. There was no time to feel self-conscious as he grabbed for the condom, tore the packet open, and sheathed himself with jerky movements. The couch creaked in protest when he moved over her, his thick erection now nudging her pussy.

She waited for the deep thrust. For the one heated stroke that would plant him firmly inside her, right where she wanted him to be, but the sudden assault didn't come. Instead he rested on his elbows, hovering over her, watching her, before moving in for a soft, sweet kiss that melted her heart.

He took the time to taste her, to let their tongues mingle, for their bodies to begin gyrating against each other, easing the weight of himself into her until they rested chest to chest.

It wasn't until she was consumed by his delicate passion, her body aching from his intimacy, that he started to tease her entrance, his length gradually nudging farther into her core.

She convulsed as he began to thrust in torturously slow motions, filling her body to capacity before retreating. She encircled his waist with her legs, biting into his bottom lip as he groaned and sunk to the hilt.

"Christ, Beth." He increased his pace.

"I want more," she breathed, matching the severity of his thrusts with her own hip undulations.

"I won't have anything more to give in a minute if you don't stop moving your ass like that."

She continued to gyrate, skimming her fingers over his back, into his hair, raising her chest to brush her nipples against his skin. As if sensing her need, he moved his attention lower, sinking his lips onto her breast to begin suckling first one, then the other. The spike of sensation was all she needed to feel the pull of her climax taking over. Fire soared through her limbs, the pleasure wrenching a sob from her lungs.

"More," she gasped. His hips began to hit hard and she dug her nails into his nape, delighting in the slap of flesh on flesh. He groaned, sucking harder, his teeth grazing her skin, the pleasure and pain almost too much to bear.

"More." She arched her back with the growing intensity. His arm snaked around her hips to grip her ass, and he ground his pelvis into her at the end of each thrust. The friction against her clit was exactly what she needed to send her over the edge.

Throwing her head back she screamed, her vision fading from white to black as he relentlessly pounded into her. He let out a strained curse, his motions becoming jerky as he came apart, thrusting deeper, harder, until he finally collapsed on top of her, resting his lips against her shoulder.

Beth floated in bliss, enjoying the heat of his panted breaths on her neck, the feel of this hard, sated man making her smile. They lay in quiet contentment, her fingers softly massaging up and down his back while she fought to stay awake.

"You're tired." His lips grazed her cheek.

"Mmm-hmm." Maybe if she rested her eyes for a few minutes she would gain her energy.

"I should go. You need to sleep."

"No," she whimpered and held him tight, unwilling to let him go.

He chuckled in her ear as his cock began to soften and leave her body. "Just give me a few seconds in the bathroom, then I'll be back."

She reluctantly relaxed her arms, keeping her eyes closed while she tried not to fall asleep. Her clothes beckoned from the floor, her insecurity compelling her to cover up, but she was too sated to move. Instead she rolled over and turned into the back of the couch, hiding the front of her body from view, snuggling into the soft suede.

When Dean returned it startled her, making her jump to awareness. Then his arms moved under her body and began lifting her. She moaned and stretched in his hold, trying to wake herself up. "What are you doing?"

"I'm going to put you in bed, then take off."

She opened her eyes, not wanting him to leave just yet. He smiled down at her, the dark lines under his eyes showing his exhaustion.

"You're already dressed," she said in confusion. Why hadn't she heard him put his clothes on?

His chest vibrated with a silent laugh as he carried her from the room. "I've been dressed for a while. You fell asleep two hours ago."

Oh no. She'd wasted their last hours together.

She frowned at him. "Why didn't you wake me?"

This morning she'd stipulated the one-day rule, but now she didn't want him to say good-bye. Their time together had flown by, moving too fast to bring any sense of satiation.

His face brightened, his smile finally reaching his eyes as he walked sideways up the stairs so she didn't hit her head. "I enjoyed watching you sleep."

She didn't want to feel embarrassed, not after what they'd shared, but she snuggled into his body anyway, now well aware of her nudity. When they reached her room, he laid her down on the quilt and helped her to maneuver underneath.

She settled into the soft mattress, lying on her side to face him with the covers pulled up to her chin. He knelt beside her and peered into her soul, his fingers tangling in the long mess of her hair.

"Oh." She sat up, tugging the quilt to her breasts. "I'll need to lock the front door after you leave."

"It's okay." He motioned for her to lie back down again. "Do you have a spare key I can take and give back to you on Monday?"

That sounded nice. The perfect ending to the almost

perfect day. Her lover had almost sexed her into a coma, watched her sleep, carried her to bed, and he also planned on locking up after himself.

"There's a key under the rock at the end of the porch, if you don't mind me staying in bed."

"Not at all, I'll head off now and let you go back to sleep."

"Okay." She hugged her pillow, wanting to ask him to stay but unsure the question would overstep this casual thing they had going.

She smiled at him while her eyes slowly closed. It required all her mental effort to concentrate on opening them again. When she did, he was leaning over her, bending in to kiss her on the forehead. Craving more from their good-bye, she tilted her chin higher. His lips drifted down to caress hers, once, twice, before gliding his tongue into her mouth.

Her insides warmed, adrenaline finally releasing into her system to awaken her senses. Before she could reach up to run her hands around his neck, he moved back.

"Sleep well, sweetheart."

She watched him leave through heavy lidded eyes that started to burn. With every departing step she wondered how long it would take her suppressed guilt to rise to the forefront and announce how stupid she'd been to sleep with her boss. Not only once, but twice.

## CHAPTER 12

*Hope you slept well, beautiful. Dean*

eth sipped her coffee and read the message again, waiting for the elevator to reach the office floor. Monday had arrived too quickly, one of her only memories of Sunday consisting of staring at her cell phone screen and reading six simple words, over and over and over again.

*Hope you slept well, beautiful. Dean*

Those twenty-nine characters had changed her plans for Sunday completely. The day was meant to be spent reflecting, to sort out the chaos of her life and figure out what to say to Mr. Sutherland about his proposal.

Instead, she spent the entire day leering at her cell, checking constantly for messages, always carrying it in her pocket. She had never been the type to concern herself with being out of reach before. Dean had changed that. Now she was obsessed, all because of one text message.

114

*Hope you slept well, beautiful. Dean.*

The only break she had all day was a phone call with Angela. Her best friend frantically ate up the gossip about Dean and didn't hide her mixed emotions.

"Just keep a firm hold on your heart, Beth," Angela had pleaded. "The number of smitten women who call through reception trying to get in contact with him is ridiculous. You don't want to be just another notch on his bedpost."

The statement had been hard to hear after she'd already convinced herself of his sincerity. Beth wanted to explain how things between them were different, unique from all those other women, but she knew how ridiculous that sounded. She had no clue what their relationship meant or what the future would bring. So she ended up accepting the advice and changing the subject.

Now Monday had arrived and she felt apprehensive about how things would pan out. She woke at the crack of dawn, her body clock still out of whack, and left for the office over an hour early.

She convinced herself if she arrived before Dean and stuck her head firmly into work mode she would be able to get through the day on a steady roll of steam. Head down, bum up, and as she took the last sip of her coffee in the elevator she ran over the to-do list in her mind.

Unfortunately, none of the tasks revolved around Dean's inviting lips or strong hands on intimate parts of her body.

The office doors were already open and the lights were on when she stepped out of the elevator. She hadn't expected anyone to be there. She couldn't hear anyone else around as she walked in, the reception area devoid of life, but when she continued down the hall to her office, she caught sight of Steve, her second in charge, walking away from her.

He didn't appear to hear her as she continued to her

office so she decided to wait until they were closer before she said her morning greeting. When he took a detour, opening Dean's office to walk inside, her curiosity piqued.

She hovered in the doorway, deciding to keep quiet for the moment while he pulled a pen from a pocket inside his jacket and began writing on the papers set out in front of him.

"Morning, Steve."

The pen dropped to the table, his bent posture immediately snapping to attention as he cursed aloud. He glanced up, his eyes widened, and his face drained of color. "Damn, you scared the shit outta me."

"Sorry."

His gaze moved to the desk and he placed his hand over the words he'd written, hiding them from view. Not stealthy in the least.

"I…umm. I had to do some reports for Dean," he offered in a rush.

On any other day she wouldn't have doubted his explanation, but with his blatant anxiety and the way he now nodded as if convincing himself of his own statement, she knew there was more to the story.

"I have an early meeting with the marketing department to go over the changes you asked for," he continued. "And Dean asked if I could come in to do these reports before he… ah…before he left to see his sister."

She frowned, not at his reasoning, but because Dean hadn't told her he was going out of town. Of course he would go to console Megan; she just thought after what they shared that he would've called to tell her as well. The thought of Steve knowing before her, though, made jealousy begin to eat away at her senses.

"He called me yesterday." He closed the drawer and moved around the desk, averting his gaze as he headed toward her. "He told me he was flying to Sydney. I was putting the reports on his desk so he could pick them up before the flight."

He also told you we had sex, she mentally acknowledged. Either that or Steve was uncomfortable around her for a completely different reason.

Dean must have been bragging. They never discussed keeping their weekend a secret, but she didn't think he would rush to tell their mutual work friends about their private affairs. Surely he wouldn't be so quick to disrespect her in front of another staff member, someone she had to supervise. Already.

Then again, she only needed to remind herself of his track record to determine the high probability. He loved to brag about his conquests, or so she'd been told.

She swallowed over the lump in her throat and faked a smile. "Okay. Thanks for the update. I'm going to get to work."

She strode across the hall to her office, her heart beating loud in her ears. Not knowing what Dean had told Steve made her nauseated. She wondered if the details would've been explicit, if her subordinate would now know of her lack of prowess or the words she'd whispered to Dean in the shower.

There was a good chance she would be the laughingstock of the office by lunch break.

Closing the door behind her, she went to sit behind her desk, discreetly watching Steve through the inner office window. He took his time leaving Dean's office. First, he walked back to take a Post-it note off what she gathered were the reports. He frowned and switched the note from hand to hand, clearly nervous. Then he screwed the paper into a ball and threw it in the bin before heading for the hall.

He pulled the door closed behind him, sparing a moment

to pointedly stare at her through the glass. She gave a nonchalant smile in return then continued to occupy herself with tidying her desk.

When he walked from view, she booted up her computer and tried to ignore the knots in her stomach. But within moments she stood from her chair and walked over to peer through the office window. She scanned the hall back and forth, and when there was no sign of anyone, she opened the door and strode confidently into Dean's office.

A sense of foreboding heightened her senses as she stared down at his desk. She shouldn't be doing this. Whatever was on that note was none of her business, but apart from the slight niggling of her conscience, nothing else stood in her way of finding out.

She reached into the bin, plucking the bright yellow Post-it from the pile of trash. Her heart thumped in the back of her throat, and her hands beaded with sweat as she straightened out the paper to read the words written in a scribbled script.

*Great score, you lucky bastard. I can't believe you
finally got her in the sack. I expect a recap of all the
sordid details when you get back.*

She blinked, over and over, the pain sinking deep.
It served herself right for being nosy.
For being such an easy lay.
For being so damn stupid.
She'd known this would happen. She'd known and yet she'd slept with him anyway.

Why? Why the hell had she deliberately sabotaged herself?

Good sex and betraying brown eyes. That's why.

On numb legs she dragged herself to the sanctity of her

office. There was no denying the note was about her. And on the slight chance it wasn't, her situation would be even worse. The thought of him sleeping with another woman over the weekend made her shudder.

Either way, the details weren't important. The damage had been inflicted. Her heart had already been shattered into a million sharp and serrated pieces.

If Dean could brag about what they'd shared with someone she had to work with, he wasn't the man she thought he was. The man she wanted him to be. The guy she needed him to be.

A sardonic laugh escaped as she began to hyperventilate. Anger and humiliation made her eyes burn. This was ridiculous. Her life these past few days was completely insane. From Max, to Dean. What other business relationship could she ruin before another day passed?

A knock at her door had her scrambling upright as she sniffed away her emotions. "Come in."

Max opened the door, his forehead creased in a scowl. "Morning, Beth." His gruff and distant tone sent a skitter of panic up her spine. "Can you meet me in my office please?"

He closed the door and strode down the hall before she could respond.

Great.

Perfect.

She counted to ten, taking in a deep breath as she tried not to freak out. He would want to talk about the proposition, and she wasn't ready. Maybe she never would be. But in her suffocation irrational state, she could see an upside to accepting Max's offer—it would piss Dean off.

He would be furious.

Livid.

Too bad she couldn't stomach the thought of taking the necessary steps to enrage him.

She left her office, wiping her sweaty palms on her suit jacket as she strode down the hall. Mr. Sutherland sat behind his desk, tapping a pen on his keyboard, his brows still creased. She couldn't remember him ever appearing so severe, his face and demeanor excessively agitated for the conversation she anticipated.

He glanced up when she stepped into his office and held her gaze for a brief second before motioning for her to sit.

"Beth." His gruff tone continued to elevate her heart rate. "I've been thinking about this all weekend and I can't find a way around it. I've tried damn hard and there just doesn't seem to be a way. And I have no clue how to say this, so I'm just going to come out and say it."

He was rambling. Max Sutherland, managing director of Sutherland & Son, didn't ramble, and the realization ramped up her panic like jumper cables to a car.

"I feel it's best if you leave your position at Sutherland & Son."

Her head jerked back in surprise. Time began to slow as a rush of blood filled her ears like a torrent of water through a cave. She could see his lips moving, but the words were broken and disheveled.

"I'm sorry…my fault…unfavorable proposition…"

The scattered pieces of conversation didn't sink in. Her mind struggled to move past the initial remark about leaving Sutherland & Son. She was beyond confused and, even if she could determine a coherent sentence, the lump in her throat felt too big to speak over.

"I need to work on my relationship with Dean."

That name broke her confusion, giving her something to focus on. Dean's name usually brought happiness from the mere mention. Now the four letters evoked determination. Frustration. She would not have her career threatened twice in as many minutes by the same man. Squaring her shoulders, she mentally dug in her heels, unwilling to let go of the position she loved.

"I don't—" She cleared her throat when the words scraped passed her throat. "I don't understand. What did I do wrong?"

He eyed her with sympathy. "It wasn't you. This situation is entirely my fault."

"So why am I being fired?" she cried and averted her gaze while tears took over her vision.

"Dean and I have had a rough past. I've done things I'm not proud of and he's never forgiven me. I don't blame him for that." He released a sigh. "But in the past year things had become easier. He hasn't been as hostile, and I was beginning to hope there may be a chance to regain the relationship we lost."

She met his eyes, the dark brown depths so much like his son's.

"I'm sorry, but I can't risk you coming between us. When I propositioned you, I didn't realize—"

"I'm not leaving my job," she seethed. "I didn't do anything wrong."

He inclined his head. "I know. I admit this situation is entirely my fault, but Dean obviously took the matter to heart. I didn't propose my intentions to you on a whim last Friday. I asked around to ensure you weren't in a relationship. I had planned on the offer to be mutually beneficial."

She cringed at his choice of words.

"I didn't realize Dean still held a grudge against me," he continued. "And that he would try to punish me for past transgressions by sleeping with you."

The air left her lungs, the noise sharp as she flinched.

Dean had used her to punish his father?

"You can't do this." She stood, concentrating hard on her glare so her tears wouldn't fall free. "It's sexual harassment."

"Sit down," he growled.

The aggression shocked her, making her slump back into her seat like an obedient puppy.

"You know as well as I do that a sexual harassment case against this company will only discredit your reputation. And I promise it's unnecessary. You will be financially compensated."

He gave her a sad smile. A placating, skin-crawling sad smile. "Look, Beth, you've been one of my best employees. And it hurts to let you go, but my son is more important. I won't lose him again. I won't make the same mistake twice. So, I plan to offer you financial compensation to leave amicably. I've also called some of my contacts and put together a list of companies who would be willing to interview you."

Willing to interview her? Did half the city know about her demise before she did?

Max speaking to people behind her back added more insult to the gaping injury. She had looked up to him for years, had admired him, and he betrayed her with ease.

The trait must run in the family genes.

"All I ask is that you agree to leave amicably and sign a statement saying you left on your own terms."

A derisive laugh escaped. A breathy, maniacal laugh. She sat there, now numb to the compiling injuries to her ego.

"When do you want me to finish?" Her voice was ragged, weak, exactly how her body and mind felt.

"I think it would be best if you left immediately. Continuing your time here will be uncomfortable and I don't expect you to suffer more because of my mistakes. Having you leave will be a big blow to the business, but that is my burden to bear. I will handle the backlash until Steve can pick up the extra duties."

She stared. Her mouth immobile, her throat too thick

with gravel, her heartbeat loud enough to cause a threatening migraine.

In the blink of an eye, her job had vanished. She was unemployed. Her financial stability grew a great big set of eagle wings and flew right out the window.

If she wasn't clinging to the last vestiges of her pride, she would have burst into chest-heaving sobs. Instead she stood, raised her chin, and left without a word, heading for the room that would no longer be her office.

She grabbed an empty archive box from her credenza and started packing personal belongings—her family photos, her lifetime supply of desk snacks, her greeting cards and personal stationery. One by one the items fell into the box, the impact of each sending a stabbing pain to her heart, until the tears stinging her eyes broke free to trail down her cheeks.

"Oh, babe, what's wrong?" Angela embraced her before she could glance up.

Beth tried to speak, opened her mouth numerous times to do so, but all that came out were broken sobs. She'd never been this humiliated and didn't know how she would admit the mistakes to her family.

Her father would be embarrassed.

Her mother would be mortified.

Shame entered the mix of her turbulent emotions. Apart from sleeping with someone she had feelings for, she hadn't done anything wrong. But that's not how it would appear to an outsider. Anyone who didn't know her high morals would judge her for being cheap and easy.

Her reputation would be ruined.

Fire burned in her veins, overpowering her shock and helping to control the rush of tears. When Angela pulled back to stare at her, she diverted her gaze, the concern in her friend's eyes enough to make her break down all over again. "I've gotta go—"

"What's going on, B?"

Fighting to gain control, she let the news out in a rush. "I just got fired." The answered gasp had her heart taking another nosedive. "And apparently Dean only slept with me to get back at his father."

"No fucking way."

She wiped her eyes hoping her mascara hadn't run. "*Yes, fucking way.*" She slammed the lid on the box and hauled it under her arm. "I've gotta get out of here. If I've forgotten anything can you please hold it for me and I'll get it later?"

"Yes, of course."

She breathed deep and willed herself not to crumple. "Okay, I'm outta here."

# CHAPTER 13

*D*ean's cock was on a hair trigger, his heart played giddyap horsey, and he couldn't help smiling at random people like he had mental issues. A guy in the bakery on his way to work had even grinned back in blatant invitation.

If he hadn't been in there to buy Beth one of the apricot Danishes she loved so much, he would've dropped the money and run. But imagining her savoring every bite like the taste was orgasmic was worth withstanding the lust-filled leer from the guy in white.

Only thirty-eight hours had passed since they were together and he already missed her. He'd spent the first two hours of the morning picturing the way she would react at seeing him. The way she would divert her eyes, a shy smile showing the faintest hint of dimples, before she unconsciously moistened those gorgeous lips with a lust-filled lick.

He would sit his ass down on her desk and watch her devour every last crumb of the Danish, enjoying their flirty exchange until he needed to leave for the airport. He didn't even need to go into the office. He just couldn't stand the thought of leaving town without seeing Beth first.

With the current level of his obsession, leaving town for the week was probably the best strategy to stop him from making a total fool of himself. He'd already decided early Sunday morning he wanted to lay everything on the line. To tell her how he felt in vivid technicolor. Removing the emotional baggage from his chest would be a welcome relief.

He swaggered into the lobby of the high-rise office building with an extra swing in his step, then froze when he recognized Delilah standing alone at the elevator doors.

She must have sensed him. Had to have. She glanced over her shoulder, meeting his gaze, and her lips pulled into a seductive curve.

"Dean," she cooed, turning toward him.

*Fuck.*

He forced his legs to continue forward as the elevator doors opened behind her, the small space now a looming death trap if he had to be stuck inside with this vulture.

"Morning, Dee."

"Morning."

She made the word sound like an invitation, the syllables holding a remarkable seductive undertone. She definitely had player skills. Maybe even better than his own. Then again, if she only wanted to play instead of latching her claws in, he would never have had a problem with her.

He didn't mind eager women. Dee simply acted obvious to the point of desperation and one night was all he had to offer her. She knew that.

The elevator closed before he could get inside and he resigned himself to making idle chitchat until the next one arrived.

"So, when are we going to hook up again?"

*Jesus.*

He masked his surprise behind a friendly laugh. Maybe harmless flirting would've been better. He certainly hadn't been prepared for the blatant come-on.

"I'm actually seeing someone."

*There.* He made the situation clear and hopefully she would realize the sex they'd shared would stay firmly in the past.

She cocked her head and looked at him skeptically. "Why do I find that hard to believe?"

He suppressed a scoff. He didn't care what she believed and let his deep frown speak volumes as he replied in an icy tone. "I'm a changed man, Delilah."

She straightened her dainty shoulders and raised her chin. "Well she's a lucky lady. Just remember—" She moved in close, grasping his bicep while she whispered in his ear. "—I'll take you any way I can. I don't care if it's a little on the side."

Had his reputation stretched so far that women thought he had no sexual morals? He clenched the brown paper bag holding the Danish in his fist. With his other hand, he grabbed her wrist and silently celebrated the perfect timing as the doors to the closest elevator slid open.

He stared at her, *really* stared at her, his lips shifting into a genuine smile as he considered his situation from a new perspective. If he committed himself to Beth, which he had every intention of doing, he wouldn't have to surround himself with women like this anymore.

He would be free to move on from his mistakes. Free from sterility.

Invigorated, he raised her hand to his lips to place a kiss on her knuckles. "Thanks for the offer, but I'm not—"

A wounded gasp drew his attention to the inside of the elevator.

Beth.

*Shit.*

She stood there clutching a box in her hands, her eyes red-rimmed, her face contorted in a mix of shock and rage as her gaze drifted between him and Delilah.

He dropped Dee's fingers and stepped back, like a fucking criminal caught in the act.

Beth stormed forward, mumbling under her breath while she bumped by him.

"Beth." Her name left his lips in a plea for her to stop.

She didn't falter, didn't even flinch. She kept striding forward as if he didn't exist.

He jogged the few steps to catch up with her and cupped her elbow. "Wait. I was just…" The words died on his lips when she turned to face him, her cheeks now streaked with tears.

"Get your goddamn hands off me."

He complied, her uncharacteristic anger almost enough to make him take a step back. He searched her face, trying to read what was happening behind those glassy green eyes, but she swung away and continued toward the exit.

What the fuck was going on?

He followed as she exited the building's glass sliding doors, the Danish still clutched in his hand. Once outside, he increased his stride, maneuvered himself in front of her, then turned and started walking backward to maintain eye contact.

"Move." She hit him with a menacing glare.

He could barely recognize her under the anger and pain. He was completely clueless to what he'd done wrong. "Talk to me."

She increased her pace, pushing her box into his chest. "Move."

"I'm not going anywhere." He stumbled over the first

descending step leading to the sidewalk, almost landing flat on his ass.

"Please, just leave me alone." Her breathing came in ragged pants, the pace of her tears increasing. She gave another halfhearted push of her box, hitting his chest with barely any impact.

Her agony tore his heart open. His inability to figure out how to fix the problem hurt even more.

Halfway down the stairs he stopped, needing to get her attention. He braced his footing and grabbed for the box, crushing the Danish in his hand. "Tell me what's going on."

With frantic, jerky movements she tried to pull the box from his grip, but he wouldn't let up. "You're causing a scene. Please, just let me go."

He stood firm, staring her down, just as stubborn and determined as she had ever been. After a few exhausted efforts to regain the box, he watched Beth's shoulders sag, the fight leaving her body.

"I hope it was worth it," she whispered.

Her eyes were tortured, sunken and glassy. He'd never seen her like this before and her reactions were hitting him like continual sucker punches.

"I don't understand." He heard his own words and hadn't realized he'd said them out loud until Beth pushed at the box.

"That makes two of us."

She attempted to wrench the box from his hands again, giving it one hard pull. He didn't have a chance to grip the edges tighter and the weight escaped his fingers. He watched in a daze as Beth fumbled with the sudden release and it fell to the ground.

A sob left her lips and he winced at the sound of smashing glass. At his feet now sat a mangled box, the lid half off to display broken photo frames and items he recognized from her desk.

He glanced back at her in confusion. She stared him in the eye and let out a weary sigh. "What did I ever do to you?"

"I—"

She turned to leave, the box still lying on the ground at his feet.

"*Beth.*"

She didn't answer his call, just continued to walk away. He glanced at the breakage in front of him, then back toward Beth as she fled. If he went after her, the box would likely be stolen, but he couldn't just watch her leave. He couldn't shake off the apprehension that she was walking from his life forever.

In the end he didn't need to make a decision. She reached the curb and opened the door to a waiting cab. She didn't even look over her shoulder, or spare a glance at her belongings as the car pulled into traffic and drove out of sight.

What the fuck just happened?

He retrieved the phone from his suit pocket and called the office, asking Angela to meet him outside with an empty box.

"Yeah, I'll get to it when I can." The usually bubbly receptionist gave him a dose of attitude, ranting about how busy the phone lines were.

Fifteen minutes and two pieces of glass embedded in his fingers later, Angela came walking out of the front sliding doors of the building. Not once in all the days of her employment had she ever greeted him with anything but a smile—until today. Now she glared at him as he hovered over the broken pieces of Beth's possessions, her facial expression making his balls shrink. Without a word she thrust the box forward.

"Thanks."

"Not a problem," she sneered.

Picking up Beth's crumpled box, he watched from the

corner of his eye as Angela turned to leave, pausing moments later before turning back to face him. "Have you ever had a heart?"

He glanced up and knew his frustration must have been evident, but she didn't seem to notice.

"I've just been pondering the thought lately."

Letting his head fall, he sucked in a deep breath. Everyone was talking in riddles. He didn't have time for this shit. He needed to find Beth and figure things out before his plane flight. The receptionist's PMS was the last thing he needed to deal with.

"What?" he snapped, reaching his limit.

"You know, pondering…like women seem to do more often than men. Does Dean Sutherland actually have a heart underneath all the layers of asshole?"

He shot her a scathing glare and raised his eyebrows, expecting more of an explanation.

"How could you bring a staff member into your petty family problems, Dean? I honestly thought you were a good guy deep down, underneath all the arrogance. Not that it's any of my business, but did you plan for Beth to lose her job when you set out to piss off your father?"

His heart clenched. Crouched on his haunches, he almost lost his balance. "What the hell are you talking about?"

She responded by increasing her laser stare of death before turning away in a huff, walking back into the building without another word.

Damn it to hell. He needed to get ahold of Beth. Pulling out his phone again, he dialed her number. He tapped his foot in a frantic beat on the cement while he prayed for her to answer. The sound of the ringing call was barely audible over the pounding in his head.

*Come on, come on, come on.*

She couldn't do this to him now. Not after the day they

shared. Not after he finally found the balls to tell her how he felt.

The call went to voice mail. Disconnecting, he dialed again...same result.

He should have told her how he felt earlier. Why hadn't he spent Saturday wooing Beth, making her see the real him, not wasting his one chance on sex and seduction?

He'd even misled her to make himself feel less vulnerable. Apart from his longtime ex, Jessica, no other liaison had taken place in his apartment. It was his rule. But sharing his space with Beth hadn't required a second thought. She had even asked him point-blank.

*So how many ladies have made the cut?*

*Too many.*

He hadn't lied. Jessica had been one woman too many, but he was stupid to have answered based on his own insecurities without thinking of hers.

Stupid, stupid, stupid.

When the third call still went to voice mail, he gave up. He didn't have much time, and he planned on getting to the bottom of the situation before he left.

Finally, Dean had laid everything on the line with his father and yet his head still throbbed like a son of a bitch. All the resentment, all the hatred and hostility over Beth being fired had spewed from his mouth like a fountain.

He'd yelled until his throat grew hoarse, while his father sat behind his desk and waited for him to finish. Throughout his tirade—which could easily have been heard by the entire office—he tried calling Beth. Whenever one call ended he disconnected and tried again.

Once his anger became containable he stopped pacing, took a seat, and listened to the calm voice of his father. Dean hadn't anticipated him taking the deep and meaningful route, but he had. The mighty Max Sutherland sat before him at the point of tears, bringing up ancient history and family issues they'd both tried to bury a long time ago.

His father wanted to make amends, to start fresh and rebuild the damage between them.

The conversation had come from left-field, completely out of the blue and he found himself unable to handle the additional drama. His father couldn't expect a rational reply. After the way his family had been torn apart Dean had no intention of making any reconciliation easy.

He ended up leaving his father's office with an ultimatum —step down as managing director of Sutherland & Son, or Dean would leave and take the majority of the staff with him.

The promise had been a senseless move, but one he planned on committing to. They couldn't work together anymore and dragging Beth into their issues had only made their relationship more unstable.

Now he raced against time and traffic to make his flight. Beth still wouldn't answer her phone, so he decided to place his efforts in a different approach.

The first three florists he called from the online directory on his phone didn't have the time to go to the extremes he needed, no matter what the cost. His hopes were now pinned on the final number in her area.

"Good morning, this is Sunflowers. You're talking with Mick."

Dean didn't want to lose his optimism, yet the snarly tone of the young man didn't leave a great impression.

"Hi, Mick, I'm hoping you can help me. I need a large

number of flowers delivered to a house in your area, and if the person isn't home I want them placed inside."

The scenario happened in the movies all the time. The hero would need to make a big romantic gesture to put him back in the game. This was his gesture.

"Ahh…you want me to go into the house when no one else is there?" The man sounded dubious and Dean could understand his apprehension.

This was the fourth florist he'd spoken to, and he still hadn't thought out the finer details of the plan. Damn it, but he was flustered. "Yeah, can you do that?"

"Is it your house?"

"No, it's not, but—"

"Dude, I can't break into someone's house. Do you know what they'd do to a skinny-ass florist in jail? Thanks, but no thanks. I prefer to keep my back-door virginity intact if you don't mind."

Dean stopped at the next set of traffic lights and rubbed his eyelids in frustration, trying not to snap his threadbare sanity. He did know the hiding place of Beth's house key but he supposed the act would still be illegal. "Okay, fine. If she's not home, just leave the flowers on the front porch. If she is there, though, I need you to tell her a message. I don't think she'll read it if you leave it with the flowers."

"Yeah, whatever."

The man's lethargy made Dean want to grab the sucker by the throat and shake him.

"Great." He clenched his teeth and pressed harder on the accelerator. "Here's what I need you to do…"

# CHAPTER 14

*B*eth arrived home twenty minutes after the incident with Dean, and for a long time afterward she didn't move from her position on the couch. She cried until her breaths came in forced gulps and every time her cell phone vibrated with a silenced call she wept a little harder.

After an hour and a half the calls stopped and the depression started to seep in. She sat quietly, her sniffles and ragged breathing the only noise filling the living room for another dazed hour and a half. Then her phone vibrated to life again.

A day hadn't even passed before her weakness for Dean kicked in. She wanted to pick up her phone and answer, hoping like a naive little girl that he would have an adequate explanation. That he would tell her everything was all a misunderstanding and his father made a mistake. That Dean would apologize for sharing the intimate details of their time together and make her understand why he'd done it in the first place.

God, idiocy was now one of her personality traits.

She couldn't comprehend how her judgment of Dean and Max Sutherland had been entirely inaccurate. They weren't the honorable men she had trusted for years. The blindfold had been removed from her eyes and the reality of who they really were became painfully obvious.

Beth had always known Dean to be a womanizer, knew he wasn't the committed type, but she always thought of him as honest. She was wrong and still couldn't believe he would be so childish and uncaring toward their friendship.

She had given him her body, let his lingering caresses sink under her skin to penetrate her heart, and in return, he only thought of her as a way to inflict pain on his father.

After her tears had dried like sand crystals on her cheeks, she decided she needed time and space to pull the shattered pieces of her life together.

The first step was to turn off her phone. For the next few days she would be a hermit.

In her own little cocoon she could be crazy—emotionally psychotic—and not give a damn about the outside world. She would allow herself three days to wallow in self-pity, eat enough double choc ripple ice cream to send her into a sugar-induced coma, then pull up the big-girl panties and get on with her life.

Her plan had been working, too, until the doorbell rang later that afternoon. She didn't have a clue who to expect. All her friends were at work and Dean would be out of town. Tiptoeing down the hall, she hoped to figure out who was there without opening the door.

A rustle of noise came from outside. A male cleared his throat. "Come on, lady."

The voice didn't belong to Dean. She released the lock and slowly pulled the door open. A rainbow of colors greeted her on the other side. A thin, blond man in his early twenties stood surrounded by bright boxes of flowers at his feet. Every color imaginable, every size and shape, and in one hand he clutched a bouquet of balloons while the other held a piece of paper.

She swallowed. On any other occasion she would have been impressed. This time, however, she just wanted to be left alone.

"Beth?" The young man raised a brow.

"Yes." She wished she lacked the conscience stopping her from closing the door in his face.

"I have a message for you from Dean."

Before he could start she halted him with a motion of her hand. She didn't want to hear a message. The hours crying this morning had been enough wasted time on Dean.

He needed to realize no words could redeem what he did. Friends or lovers, it didn't matter; you didn't deceive people you cared for.

"I don't want to hear it." She motioned for him to go away with a sweep of her hand. "Take all this stuff back, too. I don't want it either."

She began to close the door, but the little twerp stepped forward to put his foot inside the frame. He huffed in frustration while the balloons bobbed and squeaked around his head. "Look, I get paid a bonus if you listen to the message."

"Well, tell him I listened." She started closing the door again.

He didn't take the hint, leaving his foot firmly in place. "Seriously, lady, I might seem like a dude that couldn't give a crap about your love life, but underneath all this"—he motioned to his face which was now set in a scowl—"don't-give-a-shit attitude, I'm a deep and emotional guy."

She raised her brows, not impressed with his sarcasm.

"Here." He handed her the balloons.

The huge bouquet banged against the door and walls as she yanked it into the house. She didn't want the damn helium-infused display. The less she had to remind herself of Dean the better.

As soon as the guy left she would take pleasure in popping every single one of them. Better yet, she would suck the air out as she blubbered and sobbed. At least that would make her depressing situation a little humorous.

She placed the water balloon holding the bouquet together on the floor behind her, the round colorful mess taking up the width of her hallway. Dean was delusional if he thought flowers and balloons could make up for losing her job and being treated like a fool.

When she turned back to face the man, he was scrolling through his phone with the unfolded piece of paper in his other hand. He cleared his throat as if preparing to make a formal speech and she could only roll her eyes in frustration. Where did Dean find this guy?

Clenching her jaw, she stared at the man with impatience. "What are you doing?"

"I've gotta set the mood."

This was getting beyond a joke.

"Okay, I've had enough. Either remove your foot so I can close the door, or I'm calling the police."

"Wait, wait, wait." He had the audacity to hush her with his hand. "Got it." He spoke to himself while he pressed a button on his phone. In the next moment soft music echoed between them.

"Oh, for fuck's sake." She rarely swore aloud but the situation deserved an f-bomb. She recognized the first notes to the song immediately—*Unchained Melody* by the Righteous Brothers. "You've gotta be kidding me. Did Dean ask you to play that?"

"Oh no." He waved away her comment, taking a step back and straightening the piece of paper. "All part of my high-quality service." He fixed her with a snarky smile before clearing his throat again. "Beth, please give me a chance to explain. This morning was all a big misunderstanding."

If only. She wasn't stupid enough to misunderstand being fired. And then there was the retaliation toward Dean's father.

He could take his "misunderstanding" and shove it up his finely sculpted ass. She wasn't a woman who would ignore being treated with disrespect just to get another ride on his thrill drill.

She couldn't be bought. She couldn't be seduced. Well, not anymore, anyway.

Without warning she slammed the front door, locking out the world and stepping back into the sanctuary of lonely silence.

---

Wednesday morning greeted her with a brighter outlook. There would be no more tears, no more obsessive cleaning, no more alcohol or sickly-sweet ice cream. Time for pity would no longer be allowed.

Taking a sip of her coffee, she turned her phone back on. Last night she decided the best course of action would be to delete all voice messages without a second thought, which she organized immediately.

The text messages wouldn't be so easy.

There were thirty-two messages and she didn't know how to delete them in bulk without having to open them one by one. If she opened them, she would read them and seeing something from Dean wouldn't be the best thing for her right now. In the end she decided to ignore them until she regained more strength.

Next item on her agenda—call Angela to see if her belongings had been returned to the office.

"Babe, I've been trying to get ahold of you for days." Angela's tone was a mix of worry and excitement, not entirely what she expected.

"I'm sorry. I needed time to myself." Not wanting to allow the conversation to divert to a topic she wouldn't be strong enough to handle, she continued, "Do you by chance have my box of office items with you?"

"Yeah, yeah, yeah, they're here. I planned on dropping them off on the weekend, but I've wanted to fill you in on what happened after you left on Monday."

*No.*

No, no, no. Gossip was the last thing she needed, especially if the topic involved Dean. "Ange, I—"

Her friend spoke over her in a hushed voice. "You should have seen it. Dean came storming into the office like a warrior set on destruction. He slammed the shit out of his dad's door, then proceeded to yell nonstop. *All about you.* When the room finally fell silent we thought he may have offed his dad. You know, done the whole stab-him-with-his-own-letter-opener scene. Then he walked back out, slammed the door again and left, never to return. I still haven't seen him."

This was the exact reason she wanted to keep the conversation short. A tiny ounce of unwelcome appreciation nosed its way into her mind. She had come too far over the past few days to allow herself to fall back into her stupor.

"Ange, I've gotta go. If you don't want to drive over on the weekend let me know and I'll come over and pick up the box. Just message me on what you decide."

"*Wait.* There's more—"

"Thanks for everything." Before Angela could reply Beth disconnected the call.

Placing the cell phone down on the kitchen counter she went into the living room to distract herself with the television.

There would be no reruns of the conversation. She would keep herself occupied with daytime TV and make sure no more thoughts were made about her old job or the people who worked there.

Nope, not one thought would run free.

Not one single goddamn thought.

# CHAPTER 15

"What do you want for dinner?" Dean asked his sister while he drove out of the airport parking lot toward his apartment. Megan had decided to fly to Melbourne with him, taking extra time off work to relax and rejuvenate.

"Let's go to a bar or restaurant near the Docklands. That way I can walk back to the apartment when I'm tired, and you can carry on drinking until you hit your happy place… just like every other night this week." She finished the sentence in a mumble.

He let out a breath of a laugh. With a few carefully placed words his sister clearly expressed her feelings about his current behavior.

"Okay, little sis, I heard your warning loud and clear."

If only she knew of the destruction he kept hidden. He was a wreck. Lack of sleep, too much alcohol, and an unrelenting ache in his chest had morphed him into one grumpy SOB.

He'd spent the last five days trying to console his sister. Instead she turned out to be the one consoling him.

The first night he arrived at her house, he drowned his sorrows a little too heavily and ended up confiding in his sister, pouring his heart out until he passed out cold.

In response Megan took it upon herself to take care of him. In any other situation he would have told her to mind her own business, but she needed a distraction from her own pain and he was willing to be that distraction.

He already knew his sister couldn't help his situation with Beth. Megan was an angel, not a fucking magician. She couldn't make the past disappear. Beth wouldn't forgive him easily...if ever, and she wouldn't return to her position at Sutherland & Son either. Not even after his father stood down as managing director on Monday. But he would humor Megan for a while.

After they arrived at his apartment and unpacked their bags, they made the short walk to the Dock & Grill, right on the water at Central Pier. The atmosphere was quiet for a Friday night and gave them a chance to catch up on each other's lives since Megan had moved to Sydney.

"So, what are you going to do about Beth?"

Hearing her name in a soft, somber tone made his mouth dry. Taking the time to lift the last bite of steak to his mouth he chewed, pausing before he answered. "Not much I can do. I could offer her job back, but she wouldn't take it. She's too proud and independent." He shrugged, trying to act blasé when he felt anything but. "And when she won't give me a chance to explain, there's nothing I *can* do. The best thing for me is to move on."

"But you're home now. You can go to her, speak to her face-to-face. Make her listen. She's worth the extra effort, isn't she?"

Yes, he could go to her, but he'd had enough time to realize Beth deserved better. He'd known all along, and the situation with his father only cemented the conclusion. He now needed to take a step back and let her go. It wouldn't be easy. He still pictured her face in his mind every second of the day. Her soft lips, the way her eyes crinkled when she smiled, how her cheeks flushed the sweetest shade of pink when she felt embarrassed, the way…

As if conjured from his memories, Dean caught sight of a woman who looked entirely like Beth. She wore a stylish black dress which stopped at her knees, scooping low at her back, and glossy black shoes to match. He also recognized the man walking with her.

His beer hit the table with a thud as he watched one of his business rivals, William Tundall, place a hand just above her ass and open the door. He tried to convince himself the woman couldn't be Beth, and then she turned to peer over her shoulder, fixing William with a friendly smile.

Son of a bitch.

"What is it?" his sister asked.

He spared her a fleeting glance before his gaze darted back to Beth. She surveyed the room in slow motion, glancing around the occupied tables.

He held his breath, unsure what he should do. He'd spent days thinking about the moment he'd get to see her again. About the words he'd say. About the pleas he'd make.

Now he was devoid of thought, entirely frozen as her gaze landed on him.

Her mouth opened and she paused in the doorway.

He sat there, hoping inspiration would hit.

Nothing came.

He didn't know how to react, how to respond to the hurt lingering in her eyes. He kept praying she would smile. Even just the slightest twinge of her lips or a lethargic finger wave.

He needed a sign, any sign, to let him know she didn't loathe him.

But he'd never been a lucky man, and all he could do was watch as she turned and walked through the door.

"Was that her?"

He couldn't answer, didn't want to speak for fear he would choke over the lump in his throat. Instead, he gripped the table not sure if he braced himself to leave or held himself from running after her.

"You should go," Megan encouraged. "Go after her, Dean. Tell her everything you told me. Don't let her leave until she's heard it all."

His fingers dug deeper into the table, his nails protesting over the pain. He'd never chased a woman before, had never found one worth the effort. Beth's worth wasn't the issue, though. He'd go to the ends of the earth for her. He'd give up anything—everything.

But in the end could he make her happy?

Did *he* deserve *her*?

"Bloody hell," he barked and pushed from his stool. "I'll be back soon."

---

Beth increased her pace with William taking long strides to keep up beside her. She didn't know what to do. At first glance her heart had fluttered like a traitor, ecstatic to see him again, but her mind told her to run.

*Run, Dorothy, run.*

When would the see-sawing emotions stop? She couldn't stand the thought of talking to him. To stand there and listen while he tried to manipulate her and swing the situation around to make himself appear like a saint.

However, she also ached to hear his footsteps chasing after her, to call her name and beg her to stop.

The mix of hope and sadness in his eyes had made her heart clench. His acting skills were astounding. Not good enough for the beautiful woman sitting next to him to skip her attention, though. She wanted to laugh at her own stupidity. He had already moved on while she still dreamed of a flowery resolution.

De-lu-sion-al.

"You okay?" William panted in a soft voice.

She felt guilty for using him like a shield. In a short space of time the charming man had given her a brighter outlook on her future. He had previously been the product manager at Sutherland & Son, but left for a better position at a rival company. When he heard through a mutual acquaintance about her unemployed situation, he called her and offered a position with Tycana, another big-name product manufacturer.

"I'm fine." She glanced at him with a smile.

The night had been going so well. She'd agreed to meet him and his work colleagues for drinks, and for the first time in five days she hadn't felt broken.

There had been a glimmer of fun. Happiness. Those feeling of elated hope lasted until Dean filled her vision. Then it was straight back to heartache.

"You seem nervous all of a sudden. If I've made you uncomfortable by walking you out alone, then I—"

The remainder of his words fell on deaf ears as the sound of running footsteps came from behind them.

"*Beth.*"

Dean's pleading shout weakened her legs and her ankle wobbled with her next step.

"Are you okay?" William asked again.

She focused on the cab dead ahead and increased her pace. "I'm fine. I just need to get out of here."

"*Beth.*" Dean's voice was a command. "Just give me a minute to explain."

Her feet tingled in preparation to run. She never wanted to speak to him again. The wish was unrealistic, though.

If she accepted the position with Tycana, they would mingle in the same circles and were bound to see each other in the near future. She would have to face him. If not now, soon.

Damn it.

There was little point putting off the inevitable awkwardness and her shoulders slumped with the realization.

She paused, focusing on William's concerned expression as she waited for Dean to approach. "Thanks for walking me out, Will. I'll be fine on my own from here."

His gaze searched hers, his brow creased in concern. "Are you sure?"

She nodded with the best smile she could muster.

"You have my number if you need me."

She squeezed his arm. "Thank you, for everything."

William was already five feet away and heading back to the Dock & Grill when Dean came to a stop in front of her. She took a deep breath, already able to smell his seductive aftershave, and braced herself for battle.

He stood before her for a silent moment, his expression and posture defeated. The shadows under his eyes made him appear lost and she'd never seen him with stubble so thick.

He reached up, heading toward the stray lock of hair resting on her cheek. For a split second her eyes closed, anticipating the warm caress of his fingers, the heat his touch would spark in her chest.

Before he made contact and scorched her irreparably, she took a retreating step. "Please don't touch me."

A deep exhale released from his lungs and his hand fell away. "I'm sorry."

She waited in silence, biting back the questions that slammed into the forefront of her mind. What was he sorry for? Making her lose her job? Treating her like one of his easy conquests? For pretending to be someone he isn't—someone with a heart and conscience? Someone she began to fall in love with?

"I completely messed up and I know I'm an asshole, but I've worked things out with my father and you can return to work."

She raised her brows, shocked at his audacity. He was more delusional than she was if he thought she would come crawling back to Sutherland & Son after the humiliation he'd put her through.

"Wow. Thank you." There was no mistaking her sarcasm. "Is the friendly offer to sleep with your father still up for grabs, too?"

"Beth…" He glanced away, staring into the night.

The little angel on her shoulder told her to ease off and acknowledge the pain in his eyes. But the devil on the other screamed for blood. She had to regain some of her dignity after all she'd lost.

"I'm sorry to be rude, but I'll have to decline your extremely tempting offer. As much as I enjoy being treated like a whore, I think it would be better if I moved on."

His face pinched.

*Yes, I've changed Dean. I'm jaded now.*

Before the conversation had a chance to continue, she started toward the cab rank.

"Beth, I…"

When his warm hand gripped her arm, halting her movement, she almost sobbed. The pain of his touch sank deep, far deeper than skin and nerves. It buried inside her, tearing at her organs.

She turned to face him, prepared to retaliate for the agony he'd inflicted. What she found staring back at her made her pause. If all her tears hadn't been shed during the week, she would have started blubbering all over again from the despair in his eyes.

*No.*

He had no right to be hurting. He'd lost nothing while she lost everything. He still had his career; his bed was still full of eager lovers; his heart was still intact. He had no right to look at her like that. No right at all.

She twisted her arm from his grasp and pushed him away as hard as she could, slamming her fists into his chest. All the pain, all the sorrow, all the heartache released from her body in one mighty thud.

He grunted and fought for balance, his eyes now wide with surprise. A gasp escaped her lips at the shock of her own brutality, and without conscious thought, she grabbed for him. Her hands grasped his wrists, pulling them closer together as disgust began to eat away at her.

She stared into his face with shame and tried to bite back the apology resting on the tip of her tongue. He may have caused her emotional pain, but she had no right to strike out at him.

When his eyelids closed and remained shut, she didn't know what else to do except continue holding him. He seemed in need of an anchor. And no matter how much pain he'd inflicted, she couldn't stand to turn away from him.

He opened his eyes, revealing dark irises glazed in emotion. She didn't know if it was from her aggressive blow or something else, but the sight caused her own eyes to burn and a cry exploded from her chest. She needed to turn away, to mentally say good-bye to this beautiful man for good, before she lost herself completely.

He stepped into her, his arms moving from her grip to wrap around her back. He brought her into the warmth of his chest, holding her tight until she collapsed into him. His embrace felt like home, like she belonged.

It was a lie.

"No," she whispered, shaking her head, breaking free of his grasp.

"Please, just come back inside. Give me some time to explain."

Back inside where he had another woman waiting. She retreated and his hands traced down her arms until they fell limp at his sides. Closing her eyes for a moment, she savored their last touch, memorizing the gentle caress of his strong fingers.

"Good-bye, Dean."

Before she allowed a single tear to fall, she did the hardest thing she had ever done in her life. She turned and walked away from the man she loved, hoping with every broken beat of her heart that she would never see him again.

Dean slumped into his armchair, the squeak of leather breaking the silence in his apartment. His sister had been eye stalking him since he walked back into the Dock & Grill and the shadow was starting to piss him off.

He wanted to be alone, to succumb to his anger and frustration and let loose with a few stray swings at the plasterboard walls. The physical pain of a few broken knuckles would be a lot less excruciating than the suffocating band around his chest. The unrelenting throb wouldn't go away.

"So, what is your plan of attack?"

He wanted to ignore Megan and her need to fix something that was irreparable. Instead he peered out at the Melbourne skyline, seeing nothing but Beth's face in the reflection of the glass. "It's over. Just leave it alone."

"She isn't worth it then?"

His sister baited him, and even though he knew what she was doing, the deliberate jab didn't stop his head from pounding in anger. "Drop it, Megan."

"I'm just asking, big brother, 'cause frankly I don't understand. You're acting like it's the end of the world, yet here you are sitting on your butt doing nothing. You either want her or you don't. If you want her, you should stop at nothing to get her back."

His pain boiled and bubbled, making his words come out in a yell. "It's too late. She already hates me."

He tried. He called more times than he cared to remember. He'd done the clichéd forgive-me scene with flowers and balloons. And he'd even swallowed his pride and ran after her on the dock. At some point he needed to suck it up and deal.

That time was now.

"If you think about it a bit harder, you'll realize her feelings are probably the complete opposite. If you meant nothing to her, why wouldn't she speak to you? If she didn't feel just as strongly as you, she would have listened to your excuses and fobbed you off without a second thought. But to me it seems like she's too heartbroken to bear the thought of seeing you. You need to make her listen. Do some grand gesture to make her fall for you again."

"You mean some fucking Hallmark shit?" He pushed from

the chair, needing to pace out his frustrations before he cracked for good. "No, thanks."

Silence made the air thick between them, the moments passing with the *tick, tick, tick* of his kitchen clock. His sister may be the type to believe in unicorns and happily-ever-afters, but he sure as hell didn't.

He'd experienced the jagged edge of betrayal and realized firsthand that love didn't involve skipping through the park with fluffy bunnies bouncing around your feet.

If love did exist, it wasn't something that came around very often, and he doubted he would be a guy deserving of the blessing.

The time had come to concentrate on something else, to focus on his new position in the company and throw himself into his work.

Twice he'd been kicked in the stones because of love. He wouldn't be stupid enough to prolong the latest experience—or go in search of it again.

# CHAPTER 16

"*Y*ou need to sort your shit out."

Beth's eyes widened at Angela's greeting on Sunday afternoon. "Excuse me?"

"You heard me, sugar. Ain't nothing wrong with your ears. You need to sort your shit out."

Beth took a step back from the front door as Angela walked into her house. She carried an office box in her hands and without a backward glance proceeded to go down the hall.

"And what *shit* would that be?" She asked, following her so-called friend into the living room.

Angela rolled her eyes and dropped onto the couch, placing the box at her feet. "*Dean.* You know the guy whose baloney pony you were riding last weekend? Yeah, him. You need to sort him out."

Beth sighed and began to massage her forehead. "Ange, I'm not—"

"Zip it, chickadee. I don't want to hear excuses. You already hung up on me once. All I want you to do is listen, so sit down."

She ignored the instruction, too exhausted to argue. "I'm going to make a coffee. You want one?"

Angela wouldn't leave without speaking her mind but the situation would be slightly bearable on a caffeine high.

"You can't brush me off forever, but yes, of course I would love a coffee."

Beth let out a halfhearted chuckle and strode into the kitchen. The thought of Dean no longer upset her. She'd moved past that. Now his occupation in her mind only made her tired. Not just head tired, but an exhaustion that sunk bone deep, down to the marrow.

She wanted to forget him, because every minute of the day he floated into her thoughts for one reason or another. The worst part was the pleasurable memories. The good times were always at the forefront of her mind. The way he brought a smile to her face with a mere glance, how he touched her with reverence, or the way he opened up and showed a side of himself she never knew existed.

It wasn't until she found herself smiling into space that she would remember their time together had been an act.

She filled the kettle and Ange perched herself on the kitchen counter, legs hanging loose while she peered at Beth with a playful grin.

"Well, go ahead," she drawled. "Say what you're going to say."

"Okay, here goes…" Angela rubbed her hands together as if about to divulge an exciting plan. "You need to make up with Dean."

Beth couldn't even muster a laugh. "Not gonna happen."

"Just hear me out. When you told me you were fired and Dean only slept with you to get back at his father, I didn't think much about it. I mean apart from wanting to kneecap both the Sutherland men and feeling sorry as hell for you, I didn't analyze it much." Angela shrugged. "We all knew Dean was a player, so the whole sexual betrayal thing didn't seem out of character. And I assumed the wild monkey sex on the weekend had something to do with you being fired."

Ange took a deep breath. "Anyway, after the whole big barney between Dean and his father, I started thinking. Why would he go to such great lengths to make his father stand down as managing director if he didn't care about you?"

Beth's back snapped ramrod straight and she looked over her shoulder to stare at her not-so-friendly friend.

"Oh yeah, you didn't know about that, did you? Maybe if you didn't hang up on me the other day you would have learned that little tidbit sooner. So yeah, Max is leaving. I don't know all the details, but from what I can gather, Dean went majorly ape shit over you being fired and gave his father an ultimatum. Either step down and let him run the business or he'll leave. Seems to me he felt pretty strongly about his father giving you the axe."

Beth went back to preparing the coffee, turning her back on Angela to scoop the sugar into each mug. She couldn't handle the scrutiny right now. A rush of hope began warming her cheeks and she didn't want Angela to know how hung up on Dean she still was.

"Then he's been calling all week, grumpy as shit, constantly asking about you, which struck me as strange. Why would he ask about you if he didn't care? If the whole thing between you guys revolved around payback to Max, wouldn't he just move on like he has with every other conquest?"

*Conquest.* The word dampened Beth's hope and hit her with a dose of reality. No matter what Angela said, nothing had changed. Dean had still used her. Even if he did care about her job, he didn't care about her personally—in an intimate manner. The way he'd already moved on to another woman proved as much.

She finished making the coffees, stirring them slowly while composing herself. "I know you're—"

"Hold up, I'm not finished. I was already thinking the whole situation didn't add up, and then Steve starts being really weird. He's acting as if someone kicked his puppy, walking around the office with a droopy expression on his face and won't interact with anyone."

She grabbed the coffees and moved to the adjoining dining room, Angela following behind. "Steve's probably pissed because I found the note he left for Dean. His cover has been blown now, too. He isn't the well-mannered gentleman I thought he was. He's a jerk just like Dean. Both of them are obsessed with getting laid."

Angela nodded in contemplation, taking the seat opposite Beth at the dining table. "Yeah, maybe, but there's more to it. On Monday when the whole thing blew up, Steve went into a major panic. He was worried about you, worried about Dean, even worried about losing his job. But one thing he said during his headless chicken impersonation proves there is more to the story."

Beth tried not to seem eager when she asked, "What did he say?"

Angela gave her a sly smile but otherwise didn't acknowledge her enthusiasm. "He berated himself for writing the message in the first place, and then went on to say that the comments he wrote had nothing to do with Dean bragging. He looked me in the eye and told me Dean cares for you. I tried to prod him for more information but he became jumpy, saying he'd already made a mess of everything." Angela sipped her coffee and gave Beth a soft smile. "I know it doesn't prove anything but when a guy says something like that, you need to search for the hidden meaning."

Ange was right. It didn't prove much at all.

"I even tried to take one for the team," she continued. "On

Friday I offered to take Steve out for a drink. I thought maybe I could get him liquored and encourage him to talk, but he wasn't interested. Can you believe it? When was the last time we missed Friday night drinks?"

Beth sipped her coffee instead of replying. She'd be missing every Friday night drinking session from now on.

"It doesn't matter, Ange. I already know Dean's moved on."

Bright blue eyes narrowed from across the table. "How do you know that?"

"I ran into him Friday night with another woman."

Angela's mouth slowly opened. "What did he say?"

"Not much." She shrugged. "He wanted time to explain, but I wasn't willing to listen."

"Oh, honey," Angela gave her a sad smile. "I think the two of you need to sit down and sort all this crap out."

Staring into her coffee, she thought it over. She did want to hear the full story, but nothing would change. She wouldn't get her job back and seeing Dean slip straight back into womanizer mode just proved things between them were never going anywhere.

"No, I think leaving things alone and moving on would be for the best. He will be busy now if what you said about his father standing down is true. The last thing he needs is complications from me."

She felt Angela's gaze on her face while she continued to stare into her coffee.

"Do you trust me?"

The softly spoken question came from left field. She frowned at her friend and answered on instinct. "Of course."

"Well, trust me in this. You have the biggest heart I know and as your best friend I don't need you to tell me that you love Dean, I can already see it."

Beth cringed and kept her eyes busy, searching for loose cobwebs on the ceiling.

"Now, I know you're hurting and I also know you have doubts. You aren't entirely convinced that he's done something unforgivable. You're just too hurt and insecure because of his reputation to get the facts."

Damn Angela and her intuition.

"You need to think hard about how much he means to you. Are you willing to give up the chance of figuring things out because you're too scared of what he'll say? Even if there was only a ten percent chance that he could redeem himself, wouldn't it be worth it?"

Angela pushed from her chair, picked up her coffee cup, and walked around the kitchen counter to place it in the sink. "Don't give up on him because of your insecurities. Think about all the good times you told me about from last Saturday. Think about it long and hard, because once you close the door completely you may never open it again."

Beth didn't need to agree out loud. Angela knew she was right. That wouldn't make the decision process easier, though. Her heart already felt raw, each beat causing her entire chest to throb.

She couldn't handle more pain from Dean. What if he couldn't be redeemed and the situation became worse than her wayward mind had determined?

All the confusion had her closing her eyes to fight off the mix of anger and disgust in herself. She was smart; she should've figured out what happened by now. She read people well and had never been played like this before.

The situation just didn't make sense. Maybe it was all a misunderstanding and he really did care for her. Although the odds were slim, there was still the possibility that their time together last weekend had been real. Should she give him the opportunity to prove himself?

She glanced up when Angela grabbed the empty coffee mug from her hands and headed back to the kitchen. Caught in her thoughts, she hadn't noticed her friend's quiet approach. "I'm going to leave, babe, and give you some time to think."

Letting out a sigh, she pushed from her chair and followed Angela to the front of the house. At the door Angela gripped her in a bear hug and held her tight. "I don't know if it means much to you or not, but I think you should hear him out. I can see how you're hurting and you know I wouldn't encourage you to give him another chance if I didn't think something good would come of it. He just seems different, like he's hurting hard over you."

Beth nodded into her shoulder, knowing her best friend would never do anything to hurt her. Her intentions were honorable even though they could be entirely off-base. "Thanks, Ange."

Stepping back, Beth watched her friend leave. Not only had she lost Dean, but now that she no longer worked at Sutherland & Son, her friendship with Angela would slowly drift apart, too. They would no longer see each other five days a week and the time they could spend together on weekends would never equal what they once shared.

If only she could turn back time and redo last Friday afternoon. If given the chance, she would tell Max Sutherland with confidence and respect that she appreciated his offer but wasn't interested.

If only she'd had the maturity in the first place she wouldn't have lost her job, her best friend, and the man she wanted to be with.

*B*eth checked her bank balance on Tuesday morning and cursed at the numbers on her laptop screen. Instead of the usual weekly pay packet, the most recent deposit that came through that morning was larger than an entire year of her weekly salary.

This must be Max Sutherland's definition of financial compensation.

Apart from her money for annual leave and the four weeks' pay she was entitled to for not receiving notice of her dismissal, she didn't want anything extra. It was insulting. The money felt like a payoff to keep her mouth shut about the sordid details of being fired.

The situation made her angry enough to change out of her sweats into a pair of dark jeans and a vintage camisole and catch the train into town to sort the situation out. She wouldn't need to speak to Max or Dean; she would simply discuss it with Fiona in the accounting department, tell her the money needed to be returned, and figure out the correct payment she was entitled to.

Yes, she could have spoken to Fiona over the phone,

although speaking to her in person would ensure the matter was handled correctly. And okay, maybe she didn't need to wear her favorite camisole, or put on light hints of makeup to highlight her eyes, or spend fifteen minutes doing her hair, but being unemployed didn't mean she had to stop taking care of herself.

Dean would probably be out at lunch anyway, or busy taking over his father's position in the company. She wouldn't even waste her time being polite and saying hello. However, if she walked past his office and he caught sight of her, the adult approach would be to give a friendly wave. After all their years of friendship she decided the least she could do was be amicable.

By the time she reached the office building, her palms were sticky with sweat.

Stepping past the sliding glass doors into the lobby, she moved out of the way of busy office workers on their way to lunch. One of the elevators had a sign posted on the doors saying Under Maintenance, so she had more time to contemplate her stupidity for being there.

After today she would let the entire situation with Dean go. No matter what the outcome. If he wasn't in his office she would take it as a sign. If he didn't want to speak to her, she would shrug it off and move on. And if he did want to talk, she would listen.

As the elevator ascended to the fifteenth floor where Sutherland & Son held their offices, she wrung her hands together, not entirely sure she would go through with the impromptu visit.

She had always been a planner and rocking up to the office unprepared wasn't something she would normally do. The nights of restless sleep and continued heartache made it impossible for her to move on. She needed closure. Maybe seeing Dean in his working environment, self-assured and moving on without her would be enough to get over him.

When the elevator doors opened, she froze. This office felt like home and she had to swallow over the pain of now being an outsider. She found herself walking around the two other people in the elevator toward the buttons. Maybe the visit wasn't such a good idea.

"Beth?"

*Damn.*

Angela stood from behind the reception desk, taking the headset from her ears to rest on her neck as she approached. "What are you doing here?"

Good question. Beth stepped out of the elevator and pasted on a believable smile. "I have a slight pay dispute I wanted to discuss with Fiona. Is she in?"

Ange nodded, walking back into the reception area while Beth followed. "How have you been?"

"Good," She lied, making the word sound believable.

Angela's headset let out a soft beep and she placed the earphones back over her ears. "Sorry, I've got a call. Can you wait a minute?"

She shook her head. She wanted to get this over and done with before she chickened out. "I'll see you on my way out," she mouthed.

Angela nodded and pressed a button near her ear to answer the call.

Not sparing a moment, Beth walked down the familiar hall and slowed as she approached Dean's office. She walked past, pretending her intent had always been to see Fiona. Not that it mattered. His door was open and the room empty.

She guessed catching up with him wasn't meant to be.

Continuing down the hall, she arrived at Fiona's office and realized she no longer cared about being there. The pay issue hadn't been a convincing reason to travel all the way into the city in the first place. Not when she could've called. But she gave a short rap on Fiona's open door and waited for her to make eye contact before stepping inside.

"Beth, it's good to see you." The middle-aged woman stood from her chair and walked over to give her a hug. "How have you been?"

"I'm good."

Twenty minutes of chatting passed before she brought up the pay dispute. When she inquired about the business bank account details so she could transfer the money back, Fiona simply shook her head. "I'm sorry, you'll have to discuss it with Dean."

Great. She had a whole list of issues she wanted to discuss with him and receiving a payoff to stay quiet about the whole mistress sex scandal wasn't one of them.

She would write a check and hope the bank would be willing to deposit the transaction without a proper account number.

"I understand," she replied, offering Fiona a warm hug after she stood to leave. "Thanks anyway."

She didn't want to push the issue and risk Fiona getting in trouble. There was no doubt in her mind the money would be resolved in the future. She just wouldn't be discussing the issue with Dean today.

After saying her good-byes, she stepped into the hall, her mind focused on leaving Sutherland & Son without making any more heartbreaking farewells.

Maybe one day in the near future Angela could organize a night out with her old colleagues so she could see them one last time. For now, though, she needed to leave.

She had only taken two steps down the hall when her sight strayed to Dean's office door, which was now closed. Her heart skipped a beat, and then resumed pounding like a drum.

This was it, now or never. Her final chance to hear the full story.

She clenched her fists by her sides, battling an internal struggle not to run. She wasn't a child. She could ask a simple question and be adult enough to listen to the answer, couldn't she?

With determined steps she approached his office. She purposefully didn't glance through the glass panel into the room, afraid she'd chicken out at the sight of him. The sound of her knuckles tapping on the door didn't even register. Her focus was entirely on keeping her feet in place.

"Come in."

Her hand paused on the handle, and she hoped the sudden wave of nausea would recede. With a shaky hand she tightened her grip and opened the door.

The sight of him behind his desk robbed her brain of thought. His face still held the dark shades of exhaustion, and when his eyes lifted to meet hers he pushed from his chair in a rush.

"Beth." Her name was a breath from his lips and for a moment she wanted to smile.

Her traitorous body already broke out in goose bumps and the urge to rub her skin to stop the tingling was hard to resist.

To maintain her determination she broke eye contact and realized they weren't alone. Another woman sat in one of the vacant chairs in front of his desk, her hands politely clasped on her lap while she stared over her shoulder.

Beth's hand slipped from the door handle and she retreated a step as she recognized the woman's features. Dean had been with her Friday night at the dock.

"I…" Words escaped her. They floundered and jumbled in her mind. "I had a problem with my pay and wanted to discuss it with you." She glanced back at Dean, still struggling to think straight. "But it doesn't matter now. I didn't realize you were busy."

She glanced between him and the stranger. Something wasn't right. Apart from the obvious realization that he'd gotten over his inability to spend more than one night with the same woman, something kept niggling at her.

He moved around the desk, his hands coming up in a placating gesture. With each step he took forward, she took one back, needing to maintain the distance between them. The dark depths of his eyes hypnotized her, so she glanced away, looking back to the woman, who had the same hypnotizing eyes.

Oh, God.

"Beth, wait." His expression was tense, the lines of his face pained.

The lady turned her body around farther in the seat, showing the small mound of her belly through the tight material of her maternity top.

*Megan.*

The face Beth couldn't look away from was Dean's sister; she just knew it. Her face was an older version of the young girl in the photo at Dean's apartment.

At this closer view, the resemblance between brother and sister seemed uncanny. Both of them had the same face shape, dark eyes, and hair color. Both wore matching expressions of concern, as if she were a startled deer ready to flee.

She had made a major mistake in judging him the night at the dock. It seemed every decision she made through this entire unemployed and heartbroken situation revolved around immature actions.

If she hadn't been drinking the afternoon Max propositioned her, she wouldn't have taken the ride home with Dean. She wouldn't have blurted inappropriate comments. They would never have slept together.

And even more recently, she made the blunder of denying him, the chance to explain, all because she jumped to conclusions about the woman he had shared a meal with—his sister.

She shook her head at the juvenile behavior. She didn't deserve an explanation. If she couldn't allow him the chance to explain, to defend himself when she first judged his actions, did she really deserve him? Vindicated or not?

"I-I'm sorry." She spared them both a soft smile and retreated into the hall. In long strides, she fled to the reception area, berating herself with each step.

She was entirely childish. A hypocrite, too. All this time she'd been thinking of herself. *Her* feelings. *Her* betrayal.

Not once had she allowed him to explain.

He left town to be with his grieving sister and all Beth had done was make his situation worse. He'd only asked for a few minutes and she had continued to knock him back at every opportunity.

She felt entirely humiliated at her toxic behavior.

She wasn't usually spiteful or quick to lash out. She wasn't entirely untrusting either. But those reactions had come in abundance where Dean was concerned.

This person she'd become didn't deserve him. She didn't even want to face him knowing how badly she'd acted.

It was best if they forgot each other.

---

"Beth." Dean raised his voice not caring how loud the noise reverberated through the office. He didn't know why she was here, but he wouldn't let her go this time.

She didn't stop at his call. She continued through the

front office doors, not even acknowledging him after she reached the elevator and pressed the button.

He stalked after her, pausing at the doors in an attempt not to crowd her. She stood defeated, her shoulders slumped, her head drooped forward, and still she didn't turn.

He wished like hell he could simply walk over and hold her in his arms. What he wouldn't give to know what she was thinking. Her eyes had widened at the sight of Megan's round belly and he was sure she thought the baby was his.

"We need to talk." Her back expanded with a deep breath as he stepped toward her.

"No." She uttered the word and shook her head. "I just want you to know I'm sorry."

He frowned, inching closer. Their entire situation was a mess of misunderstandings and confusion. He currently wallowed in the latter, unsure why she needed to apologize.

His actions were the reason for her getting fired. His relationship with his father was the problem all along. Along with his opinion of commitment and women, too.

If only he'd recognized what he truly wanted the first time they kissed. If only he'd set his determination on having her all those months ago, maybe things would have been different.

The elevator dinged its arrival and she rushed to get inside.

"Wait." He closed the distance between him and the elevator while she stood before the operations panel, frantically tapping buttons. His blood pounded as the doors began to close, and she still wouldn't make eye contact. "*Stop.*"

He thrust his arm between the doors and cursed when they smashed into him. "Goddamn it. Please just give me the chance to explain."

He wrenched the doors apart and stepped inside to finally have those somber defeated eyes look back at him. All he could do was stare, drinking in the alluring sight while the doors closed with a clunk behind him. Over a week had passed without seeing her. A week where he had missed her like crazy.

"She's my sister," he murmured, thinking it was as good a place as any to start this train-wreck of a conversation.

One side of her lips tilted in a half-hearted attempt at a smile. "I know."

He moved toward her, close, so they were almost toe to toe. He couldn't stay away, he didn't know how. He ached to feel her, to escape in her.

"If you know, then why—"

Her soft fingers came up to rest over his lips. "I'm sorry. Let's leave it at that and move on."

Her touch burned his mouth, the sensation sinking through to his throat, his chest. He encased her wrist in a gentle grip and, kissed those gorgeous fingers. "I'm not moving anywhere until we work this out."

He reached for the operations panel and pressed the Stop button. The elevator groaned in protest, coming to an abrupt halt as alarm bells rang outside the enclosure.

She darted her gaze around the elevator, her hand falling to her side, her eyes wide, her mouth gaping. "What are you doing?"

*Staring. Salivating.*

The alarm shut off, leaving them alone in the ear-ringing silence.

"We need to talk." They needed to do much more than that, but it was a start.

Her throat worked over a heavy swallow, then finally she nodded. "I know, and I'm sorry. I should have given you the chance to explain earlier, but…"

She broke eye contact, her tongue darting out to moisten her lower lip.

"But?"

She sighed, her shoulders sagging with the exhale. "But this has become a huge mess. I'm embarrassed at how I've acted."

He traced his fingers down the side of her face and became mesmerized by the exquisite softness of her skin. She closed her eyes, letting out a barely audible whimper, and he wanted to groan in appreciation.

"I love you, Beth." The truth escaped without thought. For a split second, he wanted to retract the comment. Fear and impending humiliation had his chest restricting.

But the more he stared at her, the more he touched her beautiful skin and breathed in her sweet scent, the more he didn't care about the consequences of his admission.

He *did* love her and he didn't care if she shot him down in flames; he needed her to know the extent of his craziness for her.

"Don't." Her eyes squeezed tighter, her palm moving to rest on his chest in a punishing attempt to push him away.

"Let me explain," he whispered. "Please."

She opened her eyes. "I don't deserve an explanation. Last Saturday meant everything to me. You gave me a glimpse of the real you. I got to see a side of Dean Sutherland that I never knew existed. And God, it made me happy. But then Monday came and I was blindsided by—"

"I know, and—"

She placed her hand over his mouth and smiled. "Let me finish."

He raised a brow, impressed and slightly turned on at her sassy demand.

"Dean, I was blindsided by a note that Steve wrote about us. Knowing you'd told him intimate details about our time together really hurt me. Then the things your father said made it worse. I couldn't think past the betrayal to give you the chance to explain. But I shouldn't have been so quick to judge you after the weekend we shared. And I'm sorry for that. I not only made the situation worse for you while you were out of town helping your sister, but now I look like a childish brat."

He smiled under the weight of her palm. No other woman would apologize for giving him the cold shoulder after what she'd been through. Not under those circumstances.

He kissed her palm and grasped her hand, moving it away from his mouth. "Brat or not, I kinda like the way you look."

She gave a halfhearted chuckle and the flicker of warmth in her eyes spread through their connection, up his arm, into his chest. "You 'kinda like' a lot of things."

He couldn't help smirking at the memory of the hysteria on her face the first time he'd said those words to her. "Only with y—"

A loud bang sounded from the elevator shaft above, making them both jump.

"This is building management," a man's voice boomed from overhead. "Is everything all right in there?"

*Damn it.*

All Dean needed was five more fucking minutes.

He tilted his head toward the ceiling, so he didn't shout in Beth's face. "Yeah, we're fine. Just give us a sec."

"I'm sorry, sir, but unless there's an emergency, I'm going to need you to return to the lobby. We've had technical difficulties with the other elevator and this is the only one available. We have a large group of people trying to get back to work after the lunch break."

"Yeah, okay." He bit back a growl. "No problem."

He returned his attention to Beth, ignoring the building manager's request. He couldn't risk her leaving without hearing him out and he still had a mass of things to explain.

"I need you to understand the situation with my father. You have to realize I didn't sleep with you to get back at him. His proposition only spurred me to do what I should've done a long time ago."

Her brow furrowed, her gaze narrowing with the slightest skepticism. "What does that mean?"

"It means I haven't been able to stop thinking about you since the first day we met. You were everything I made myself believe didn't exist—honest, passionate, loyal, dedicated."

He stepped into her, joining their bodies thigh to thigh as he stared down at her. "I could go on for an eternity listing your attributes and still not convince you of everything I admire. But the main point you need to understand is that I always thought you were too good to be true."

She balked and he loved the innocence of her response.

"I always thought you weren't entirely real," he admitted. "At the very least, you were too pure and sweet for a guy with my reputation. Then we kissed at Onyx and everything changed. From the instant our lips met, I needed more. But you left without a word and acted as though you regretted every moment."

"No." She shook her head. "It wasn't like that."

He moved close, their mouths a breath apart as he clucked his tongue. "Now it's my turn to explain. Okay?"

He kissed her, a slow, soft swipe of connection. "After Onyx I was gutted. Your rejection cut deep and for once I lacked the confidence to go after what I wanted. It wasn't until my dad set you in his sights that I knew I had to do something. But it wasn't a father-son rivalry. Not exactly. I've never seen you date. Not even once. So, the thought of losing you to anyone was my motivation."

He paused, trying to judge her reaction. Her expression

gave nothing away. No belief. No skepticism. She held herself in check, perfectly composed.

"I would never use you." He marked his words with another brief kiss. "I would never disrespect you."

"Then why did you brag to Steve about us?" she whispered against his lips.

*Shit.* That stupid note.

"I didn't give him intimate details." He broke eye contact to nuzzle his face into her neck. "I merely told him we were together, and I did it for two reasons. The first, I admit is childish. I couldn't keep the news to myself. I needed to tell someone, and Steve has known how I've felt about you for a long time."

She wriggled in his arms, attempting to break free, but he held her tight.

"The second reason—the *main* reason—was because I wanted him to take care of you while I was gone. I told him about my father and how you would be uncomfortable coming to work on Monday. I needed to make sure I was kept in the loop if anything happened. It was the only way I could drag myself out of town when I knew Megan needed me."

Her body sagged into his and he took it as a sign of acceptance. He caressed her cheek with the tip of his nose, moving his mouth down to place a kiss on the sensitive flesh below her ear. "There haven't been any other women. There's only you."

"I want to believe you."

"Believe me, Beth." He closed his eyes and slid a hand under her camisole, his fingers lightly gliding over the skin of her lower back. "I'm drowning in you."

Dean's hand slid through her hair, his large palm cupping her head while his mouth returned to hover over hers. The beat of his heart thumped against her fingers as those dark brown eyes devoured her.

And he thought he was the one drowning?

She swallowed to alleviate her parched throat and the compulsion to lick her lips was undeniable.

His mouth inched closer. The rush of eager anticipation flowed through her ears, making her oblivious to anything else but him. A faint noise skittered into her subconscious, the interruption not resonating. The touch of his hands demanded all her attention with their delicious stroking.

His lips brushed hers, a delicate sweep of perfection.

"Sorry to ruin the moment—" She jumped at the loud voice booming from above them. "—But if you don't start the elevator now, I'm going to have to call the police."

Her eyes widened in a mix of embarrassment and amusement while Dean grinned down at her.

The noise now came from right above the door. The building manager must have located the level they were stuck between and came closer to investigate.

"We better go."

Dean shook his head. "Just a few more minutes."

His lips moved over hers before she could protest. The brush was delicate over her building smile, before he pressed further for a deeper kiss. She sank into his chest, a moan leaving her throat while a gentle tongue stroked hers.

"Come on, guys," the man pleaded. "The lobby is like a mosh pit."

She chuckled, overwhelmed with a sudden sense of happiness. Dean didn't let her go. He moved a hard thigh between hers, stepping forward to rest her against the wall.

With seductive force, he tasted her, his tongue thrusting, his thigh grinding, his hand gripping her hair.

Every inch of her tingled. Throbbed. She ran her hands along his chest, around his neck, wanting more, just the slightest bit to sate her insatiable need.

His fingers along her scalp made her tingle. Each stroke, each thrust, each lick made her delirious.

"You do realize we have a camera in the elevator," the man shouted. "As we speak, my assistant is in the control room watching the two of you."

Oh, God.

She'd made another bad decision—coming to her old job, approaching Dean, making out in a stopped elevator while being recorded... But this time her punishment didn't come in the form of heartache. Her eyes burned with happiness. Her stomach tumbled with rapidly amassing butterflies.

Dean snapped to attention, his heated glare fixing on the small dome camera in the back corner. With a growl he slammed two knuckles against the lobby button.

She had to press her lips tight to hold in hysterical laughter, at least until the elevator lurched into movement, making her gasp.

"It's okay." Dean grabbed her hand, his thumb stroking back and forth against her skin as they descended.

When the doors opened on the ground floor her cheeks burned hot. People were banked up five deep around the door. Some of them frowned, shooting her filthy looks, while others held cheesy grins as if they pictured what sort of triple-X action had been going on in the elevator.

Dean led her through the crowd, out into the open space of the lobby before he stopped and turned to face her. Those dark eyes read her, the gentle tweak of his lips increasing her euphoria as he leaned in to curl her toes with a sweet kiss.

She grinned against his mouth, not caring they had an

audience—until he pulled back and lowered to one knee at her feet. Her stomach descended with him, leaving her body and falling straight to the floor. This couldn't be happening. He couldn't be proposing.

She scanned the room, frantically searching for a distraction, a lifeline, anybody or anything to stop another train wreck.

"Beth, I've missed you. I can't stand waking up—"

"Dean," she warned, still searching for someone she knew in the crowd of people who were now turned in curiosity, eager to watch the unfolding disaster.

"—and not seeing your face at work every day. I want to get to know you better—"

"*Dean,*" she pleaded, her hand pulling at his in an effort to make him stand. She began to rub her neck with her free hand, trying to ease the tension so she didn't hyperventilate.

"I want you in my life—"

*Oh, God.* "Please, Dean."

He ignored her. Surely the horror must be clear on her face.

"Will you go out with me?"

The room went silent, or maybe her ears just stopped functioning.

What did he ask? She frowned, trying to rerun the conversation while a smirk brightened his face. Not will you marry me but *will you go out with me?*

She dropped his hand and glared.

*Bastard.*

She tried to convey how much she wanted to flay him alive while she pressed her lips tight, determined not to smile. "You scared me half to death."

His smirk transformed into a grin, a set of gleaming white teeth hitting her full force. No woman in her right mind could have resisted smiling back at the beautiful man kneeling before her. She didn't need to turn and see the faces of the women onlookers to know they were wondering why she was so lucky.

"I suppose asking someone on an actual date is as monumental as proposing marriage for a player like you," she drawled.

He clutched at his chest, feigning a mortal injury. "You're killing me, sweetheart."

She glanced around, taking note of the tens of people smiling at them, their faces eager as they waited for a conclusion. "You know everyone thinks you just proposed, right?"

He gave a smug nod. "Are you going to let us all know your answer?"

He reclasped their hands, his touch sending warm tingles through her arm and down into her chest. She should continue glaring. He didn't deserve to be let off the hook so easily. Not when the gossip of this moment would take minutes to shoot through every level of the building, and years to leave.

But those dark eyes, that perfect smile, his gentle touch... They warmed her in a way she'd dreamed about since she first met this man.

Their future had been mapped out in her mind through thousands of fantasies for the longest time. The one thing that always seeped in to ruin the image was Dean's reputation and the fear he couldn't commit.

His face fell, the mischievous smile disappearing as if he understood her thoughts. He continued to gaze up at her from his position on bended knee, not once allowing his attention to waver to the crowd standing politely out of hearing distance.

"Beth." His eyes pleaded more than his words as he clutched her fingers tight. "I love you."

The world tilted, her vision skewing for the briefest second.

He had said those words in the elevator, but back then she hadn't listened. She hadn't deserved to hear them. She hadn't wanted to believe him.

This time was different. This time his heart poured into the three monumental words, his honesty weaving around her, comforting her.

"Beth?"

She couldn't deny him.

Her head nodded in enthusiasm and she mouthed her answer without voice. The lobby erupted in a mass of cheers, the outside world beginning to spin again. The crowd may think they were now engaged, but that didn't matter. Dean's dating proposal had been just as monumental as a proposal of marriage. And she couldn't be more elated.

He loved her. Dean Sutherland, woman-slayer of the city and surrounding states, loved her. Her heart soared on a high while she tried to contain her emotions.

Moving to his feet, he wrapped his arms around her and she closed her eyes in his embrace.

"I love you," he whispered. "God, how I love you."

THREE MONTHS LATER

Beth raised her brows and stared down at Dean who was lowered on one knee before her. Really? He was really going to repeat the whole fake proposal again?

She mentally recounted how many times he'd played this stunt. The first time had been to ask her out on a date. The second came at the end of the first date, his bended-knee request for a second date this time. Then the third scene had been at a random park only two weeks later, asking her to return to her old position at Sutherland & Son.

The most recent, and monumental, had only been last week, on the balcony of his apartment—Will you move in with me?

Yes, his bended knee proposals were moving up in slight degrees but he'd done them so many times that the zing had now left the building.

"Dean, if you ask me something lame like if I want

Chinese for dinner, I'll have to remove your manly bits with my fingernails."

The smile he shot her contained pure, intoxicating heat with an even more impressive dose of affection. After three months, she still hadn't become used to his intoxicating devotion. The way his eyes filled with appreciation and adoration caused her heart to skip a beat every damn time.

"No, sweet cheeks, this isn't about Chinese, so please take your eyes off said manly bits."

Well, that deleted one possibility off a list of thousands.

She shook her head in exaggerated frustration and turned to walk away. She loved him to death, but she didn't have time for another fake-proposal re-run when there were a billion stacked boxes littering his hallway.

Although, she would never admit it out loud, the decision to move her belongings into Dean's home without profes-sional help had been a mistake of monumental proportions. She'd imagined salivating over her man's sweaty, sexy body all day and instead she'd been too distracted with lower back pain from all the heavy lifting.

He grabbed her hand before she could flee and held tight. "Please, Beth."

A smile tugged at her lips. She couldn't deny him. Not in the bedroom. Not in the office. She gave him everything he wanted, and he returned the generosity tenfold.

She turned toward him and gasped at the sight before her.

His grin remained intact while he clutched her fingers in a warm, gentle grip, but his other hand now cradled a small black box.

She closed her gaping mouth and tried to remain calm as she raised a brow. She could play it cool. That box was more than likely filled with a key to his apartment. The small, black velvet jewelry store box he deliberately used to try and tease her out of her ever-loving mind.

"Beth Graison." He released her hand, his gaze never leaving hers as he opened the box with a deafening creak, then reached for her again.

She tried to ignore the glimmer coming from his open palm, tried to keep her eyes locked on his while little bursts of reflected light beckoned to her.

"You've ruined me," he murmured. "There will never be anyone else. Not now, or in the future."

A sob escaped her lips and her heart palpitated at a salsa rhythm. She couldn't think. Couldn't form words.

His expression softened, his smile losing its male arrogance to be replaced with the adoration she'd grown addicted to. "I love you. I didn't even fully grasp the concept until we first kissed, and now I would die before letting you go. Will you do me the honor of becoming my wife?"

She swallowed, her brain still malfunctioning. There was no response for this moment. Nothing monumental or exquisite enough to mark this occasion. Tears burned her eyes, the sting causing her to rapidly blink her blurring vision. "I-I…"

She grasped at his hand, pulling and tugging until he raised to his feet. She flung her arms around him, clinging tight as she nuzzled into his chest.

He held her until her pulse slowed to a pace where she could breathe. Held her as if he would never let her go. Held her until he finally whispered in a panic, "That's a yes, right?"

She pulled back and stared into the future happiness she could easily read in his eyes. "Yes, Dean Sutherland," she choked. "I want nothing more than to marry you."

---

*THE END*

# ABOUT THE AUTHOR

Eden Summers is a bestselling author of contemporary romance with a side of sizzle and sarcasm.

She lives in Australia with a young family who are well aware she's circling the drain of insanity.
Eden can't resist alpha dominance, dark features and sarcasm in her fictional heroes and loves a strong heroine who knows when to bite her tongue but also serves retribution with a feminine smile on her face.

**If you'd like access to exclusive information and giveaways, join Eden Summers' newsletter via the link on her website - www.edensummers.com**

*For more information:*
www.edensummers.com
eden@edensummers.com

www.ingramcontent.com/pod-product-compliance
Lightning Source LLC
Chambersburg PA
CBHW050408190726
48284CB00007BB/2485